OLD BONES CAN BE MURDER

Connie Shelton

Books by Connie Shelton
THE CHARLIE PARKER MYSTERY SERIES
Deadly Gamble
Vacations Can Be Murder
Partnerships Can Be Murder
Small Towns Can Be Murder
Memories Can Be Murder
Honeymoons Can Be Murder
Reunions Can Be Murder
Competition Can Be Murder
Balloons Can Be Murder
Obsessions Can Be Murder
Gossip Can Be Murder
Stardom Can Be Murder
Phantoms Can Be Murder
Buried Secrets Can Be Murder
Legends Can Be Murder
Weddings Can Be Murder
Alibis Can Be Murder
Escapes Can Be Murder
Old Bones Can Be Murder - a novella
Holidays Can Be Murder - a Christmas novella

THE SAMANTHA SWEET SERIES

Sweet Masterpiece   *Sweets Begorra*
Sweet's Sweets   *Sweet Payback*
Sweet Holidays   *Sweet Somethings*
Sweet Hearts   *Sweets Forgotten*
Bitter Sweet   *Spooky Sweet*
Sweets Galore   *Sticky Sweet*
Sweet Magic

Spellbound Sweets - a Halloween novella
The Woodcarver's Secret

THE HEIST LADIES SERIES
Diamonds Aren't Forever
The Trophy Wife Exchange
Movie Mogul Mama

CHILDREN'S BOOKS
Daisy and Maisie and the Great Lizard Hunt
Daisy and Maisie and the Lost Kitten

Old Bones Can Be Murder

Can Be

Murder

Charlie Parker Mysteries, Book 18.5
A Between-the-Numbers Novella

Connie Shelton

Secret Staircase Books

Old Bones Can Be Murder
Published by Secret Staircase Books, an imprint of
Columbine Publishing Group, LLC
PO Box 416, Angel Fire, NM 87710

Book layout and design by Secret Staircase Books
Cover images © Unholyvault, Destina156, Ayutaka

First trade paperback edition: March, 2020
First e-book edition: March, 2020

* * *

Publisher's Cataloging-in-Publication Data

Shelton, Connie
Old Bones Can Be Murder / by Connie Shelton.
p. cm.
ISBN 978-1945422874 (paperback)
ISBN 978-1945422881 (e-book)

1. Charlie Parker (Fictitious character)—Fiction. 2. New Mexico—
Fiction. 3. Great Britain—Fiction. 4. Women sleuths—Fiction. I. Title

Charlie Parker Mystery Series : Book 18.5.
Shelton, Connie, Charlie Parker mysteries.

BISAC : FICTION / Mystery & Detective.

813/.54

As always, I have a huge amount of gratitude for everyone who helped shape this book into its final version. Dan Shelton, my husband, helpmate, and expert on all things helicopter—I couldn't do it without you. And thank you Stephanie, my lovely daughter and business partner.

Stephanie Dewey, Shirley Shaw and Marcia Koopman—thank you for dropping everything to read and catch the typos that sneaked past me.
You guys are the best!

Chapter 1

It all started with a Chinese fortune cookie message: "A close relative needs your help." I phoned each of my brothers—both were doing fine. My husband Drake was sitting across the table from me at Ming's. He didn't seem in any particular distress, but I asked anyway. A shake of his head as he took the last bite of his shrimp fried rice.

"These things are dumb," I said, wadding up the scrap of paper and adding it to our trash pile of throwaway chopsticks.

We went for a drive, the scenic route through Albuquerque's north valley, went home and got naked together, since it had been a few days. It wasn't until I went to the kitchen later in the evening, with a hungry spaniel at my heels, that I spotted the blinking light on the answering machine. I swear, we use our landline so seldom any more, I forget there are still a few people who aren't trying to sell us something, the ones who'll actually leave a message.

"Charlie, dear, it's your aunt Louisa." Her British-accented voice came through clearly. "I've been thinking of you quite a lot recently. Do give me a ring."

My father's sister, my namesake aunt. I hadn't known of her existence until a few years ago when a letter came, out of the blue, and I'd taken her up on the offer of a visit. She was one of the most interesting women I'd ever met, with an extraordinary life of travel and experiences to her credit. American born, she'd settled in England several decades ago. I calculated the time difference. It would be incredibly early in the morning in the UK, and my aunt was no pre-dawn riser—I recalled her as much more a night owl.

A close relative needs your help.

A whine at my heels caught my attention. Freckles was the reason I'd come into the kitchen in the first place, and she wasn't happy her dinner was coming so late. I scooped kibble into her bowl as I pondered Louisa's call.

I played the message again, listening for nuances in her tone of voice. Could she be in some type of trouble? This one had come more than a day ago, and her voice sounded normal.

I swear I do not place any credence in fortune cookies but this one was weird. They usually say things like you'll have a long and happy life, or a windfall is coming your way. But to say that someone needed my help? What if that cookie had been specifically meant for me? I couldn't ignore the possibility.

While the dog lapped noisily at her water bowl, I

padded barefoot back to the bedroom. Drake was curled up under the covers, deep in a satisfied sleep. I wrapped my robe more tightly around me and found a pair of cozy slippers. At my desk in our home office, I began searching online for flights to London. No harm in checking prices and availability.

Two hours zipped by, as they tend to do when I'm at the computer. Freckles had dropped a ball at my feet repeatedly, but she finally gave up when she got no response from me. I certainly wasn't going to head off to the park at ten p.m.

By eleven, I had checked ahead on Drake's calendar to be sure there wasn't a job coming up that would require me to be there. And I'd automated most of the duties at my regular job as accountant for RJP Investigations so I could take my laptop and handle the few end of month chores from anywhere, including Aunt Louisa's tidy little home across the pond. I had to admit I was getting excited about the prospect of a trip, even if it meant I might be going there to jump into some kind of family crisis.

Back in the kitchen I listened to her message once again. She'd said only that she had been thinking about me recently. I was probably getting way ahead of myself in planning a visit. At least it would now be after seven in the morning for her, a time I could decently call without alarming her, not *too* much.

I began by apologizing for the early hour.

"Oh, Charlie, it's fine, absolutely fine. I was up and putting the kettle on." But I could hear her yawn through the connection.

"Is everything all right?" I asked.

"Quite. Spring was lovely and the summer is shaping up quite well. I'm still doing my tours. Oh! Next week I'm attending a symposium in London on the role of ghostly beings in crime detection. Wouldn't it be marvelous if you could come!"

Aunt Louisa gives nighttime tours of the haunted sites in her small town. I could easily see how any conference on a ghostly topic would grab her attention. Kitchen sounds came through—water filling her electric kettle, the clink of a mug.

"Actually, when I got your message, my first thought was how nice it would be to visit again," I admitted. "I haven't run the idea past Drake yet. It's the fire season here in New Mexico and it could be that he'll be away for several weeks anyway."

My mind was racing. There would be a lot of details to manage—what to do with Freckles if we were both gone at once was a main one. Was my passport up to date? How much more would an airline ticket cost on short notice?

She was going on about the program and the dates of the symposium, and I jotted them down as these other thoughts ran through my head.

"I've booked my room already," Louisa said. "You could fly into Heathrow, get the train into central London, and share my accommodations. A girls' trip to the city. How brilliant!"

I reiterated that I had a lot of details to work out, but I had to admit her enthusiasm was contagious. I promised to get back to her within a day or so. By the time we ended the call it was well after midnight and I suddenly wasn't the least bit sleepy.

As I feared, the plane ticket was a bit of a shocker on a last-minute itinerary, but I had some savings and decided the splurge would be fun. I put a ticket on hold for the last seat on the only flight that would get me there while Louisa was still in London. I wouldn't make the conference dates, but she would fill me in if I expressed an interest. It was more the prospect of hanging out with my vivacious aunt that appealed anyway.

Finally, I tucked into bed beside Drake. Too many thoughts kept me from falling asleep, but I had eight hours to confirm my flight. I could let him get his sleep and break this startling bit of news in the morning.

As my eyes drifted shut at last, my final thought was at least Louisa had not been in dire need of my help with something. Silly fortune cookie.

Chapter 2

I'm a little jealous," Drake admitted over breakfast that morning. "Your aunt sounds like a fun person to spend some time with."

"Then come with me," I said, belatedly remembering I was holding onto the last ticket on the flight.

He patted my hand across the table. "Nope. You do it."

"You're sure? We can find a schedule that'll work."

"I hadn't mentioned it yet, but I had a text this morning from Ben Hernandez at the Forest Service. Looks like they're going to send me to a fire down in the Gila. I was waiting to tell you about it before I confirm with him, but I really should take the job. You know how that goes every year. Until the monsoons, these fires are going to start up. I need to be ready."

He didn't mention that the long hours and months of

work provided a big chunk of his income for the year too. If he wasn't here to take the job, the Forest Service would assign it to someone else, possibly an out-of-state operator.

"You don't mind my being gone for ten days?"

"Work out some arrangement for the dog," he reminded. "I can't take her with me. Dump the rest of your obligations and just go—you'll love it."

The rest of my obligations meant my partnership with my brother at RJP Investigations, and Ron already knew that I would take off anytime I wanted. As long as the clients received and paid their bills, he didn't much care about the rest of my duties there.

I picked up my phone and retrieved my airline reservation code, booked the flight, and swallowed hard as the charge hit my credit card. Once that was set, I texted Victoria and asked if they would like a canine visitor for a while. My sister-in-law absolutely adores our little brown and white spaniel-mix. Unless they had travel plans of their own, I couldn't imagine her turning me down. But, if they couldn't manage it, there's a great boarding kennel nearby and Freckles has done quick overnight visits there a few times.

Within moments, however, the phone pinged with Victoria's reply: **Yes! We'd love to have her!! (smiley face)**.

"Looks like I'm going to England," I told Drake as I cleared the dishes. I tried to make it seem as if this was a big favor for my aunt, but truthfully in my head the phrase was coming out in a joyful sing-song: *I'm going to England … I'm going to England …*

He planted a kiss on my forehead before heading to the bedroom to don his flight suit. He'd responded to the Forest Service request while I finalized my own travel arrangements. From the parts of the conversation I caught, he needed to report for a check ride this morning and to complete some paperwork so he could be ready the moment he was needed.

I loaded the dishwasher with the breakfast dishes and caught a glimpse out the kitchen window of my neighbor Elsa Higgins and her caregiver Dottie Flowers. No time like the present to check in with them. After Elsa's heart attack last fall Dottie had moved in, a wonderful angel in the form of a large woman who was ideally qualified to care for a spunky ninety-year-old. A month ago, the two had set out tomato plants and some other vegetables. Now, it looked as if they were studying the progress of the tiny green peaches on one of Elsa's fruit trees.

I wiped my hands on a towel and opened the back door, letting Freckles run past me. The moment she heard their voices, she dashed for the break in the hedge between our two properties.

"Hey, you two. How's it going?" I asked once I caught up.

"Well, isn't this just the most beautiful day?" Dottie asked. Her dark face lit up with the kind of joy only a natural born gardener can find in the fact that she was bent over plucking weeds from between the bell pepper plants.

"We'll have quite a crop of peaches by this fall," Elsa added. "Look at these branches."

"What's new with Miss Charlie?" Dottie asked, straightening and noticing my expression.

"Well." I took a deep breath. "I've been invited to England."

"Going to visit Louisa again?" Elsa asked.

"Exactly. It's super short notice, but I think everything's all set. Drake will probably be away on a fire contract, but

Ron and Victoria will watch Freckles. So, if you could just—"

"You don't gotta send Freckle-baby away," Dottie said. "She more than welcome to stay right here with us. Right, Miss Elsa?"

"Oh, I hate to ask …" I began.

"No trouble at all," Dottie said. Under her breath she added, "Dog's good company. Keeps Miss Elsa young."

"I heard that. It's my heart that went bad, not my hearing."

"What do you think, Gram? It wouldn't be too much to have a dog around?" My sense of imposing battled my need to do the best for all concerned.

In the end, we came up with sort of a shared custody arrangement where the dog would stay with Elsa and Dottie most days; Victoria would step in on Dottie's bowling night and her day off or as the need might arise. I couldn't possibly worry too much—my baby was in the hands of those who would love and spoil her the most.

The days flew by as I decided what clothing to pack, made a travel bag for Freckles and one for Drake, saw my husband off for his own adventure, and got myself to the airport. The flight was long—there's no way around that part—and when I arrived at Heathrow it was only due to the innate courtesy of the British airport greeters that I found my way to the train heading toward central London.

By that point I would have dozed but was too keyed up and worried over missing my stop. Growing up in New Mexico doesn't really prepare a person for the reality of public transportation and navigating around a huge city. We simply hop in our cars and drive to wherever we want to go.

But I managed it all, and when I saw Louisa's smiling face at Victoria Station my stress evaporated.

"My girl, you look radiant," she exclaimed, a little loudly. She wore loose purple cotton pants and a turquoise and lavender print top that floated in gentle folds around her slightly generous hips.

"I do not. I look travel worn and jet-lagged." I laughed and she hugged me.

"All right, it's true. You are a bit ragged for the moment. We'll get you to the hotel and then a decent lunch. If you can stay awake most of the day, you'll settle in better in the long run."

"I think I can manage it."

"So, our hotel's not far. Can you handle a ten-minute walk? I'll pull your bag, if you like."

"The exercise will do me good. There's nothing like twelve hours in an airline seat to make a person want to get out and moving." I took the suitcase handle myself.

"Splendid." She turned toward the exit doors, her quick movements reminding me of her spritely demeanor.

With her wavy, shoulder-length blonde hair and the wispy fabrics she favored, plus her quick movements and vivid hand gestures, I doubted anyone would guess her age was well into her sixties. She moves and acts younger than I do. And she'd certainly used her years well, traveling the world and making the most of her life. I must admit to having somewhat of a girl-crush on her.

We stepped out into a mix of the historical and the modern—Victoria Station, with its red brick and stone façade, and in the next block a modern pharmacy next to a clothing store with windows filled with the latest fashions. Teens with nose rings and tattoos passed us without a glance, on their way to the historic station dating back to 1860.

Our hotel sat on a quiet side street, an edifice of white stone with small columns flanking the entrance. A glossy black door led into the small reception space, where Louisa greeted the clerk with familiarity. I had learned this about my aunt during my last visit—she tends to become friends with everyone. We stepped into a tiny, two-person lift.

"I've been using the stairs," she explained as she studied the buttons. "Always trying to get my exercise. But with the luggage …" She pressed a button and we rode to the third floor.

The room was slightly cramped with two beds and an armoire, but the linens were plush and comfy looking. A desk held a kettle and the standard tea setup with cups, saucers, teabags, and small packets of cookies. A tall window faced the street and filmy sheer curtains reflected the light.

"So how was the symposium?" I asked as I stashed my undies and folded T-shirts in the drawer she'd left empty for me.

"Oh, it was quite enlightening. The dead most definitely can tell us things. Prasha Bhaktari was the most fascinating of the speakers—maybe you've read her book?"

I had to admit I hadn't; actually I'd never heard of the woman who was apparently an authority on ghosts at crime scenes.

"Her work could come in handy in your private investigation business," Louisa called out as I headed into the bathroom to put away my toiletries.

I laughed. "I'll mention it to Ron, although we mainly handle employment background checks and the occasional philandering spouse these days."

"Well—I promised you some lunch," Louisa said when I emerged. "And I have just the place. Have you ever shopped at Harrods?"

"Never. But I would love to check it out." Of course I'd heard of the famed department store where a person could supposedly buy anything in the world. Most likely that was true when there was a lot less stuff in the world—and before Amazon, of course.

We gathered our purses and headed down the stairs. "It's a bit of a walk," Louisa said. "I'd recommend a taxi." And she proceeded to flag down one of the ubiquitous boxy black things I'd so often read about in novels and seen in British movies. Today's version seemed smaller as it pulled to a stop at the curb, but inside it was amazingly roomy and we settled in as Louisa told the driver where we were going.

"Quite the heat wave," he commented, steering into the traffic.

Louisa agreed. Apparently, it was unseasonably warm for June in Britain, although it felt pleasant enough for this girl from the desert Southwest. The discussion between cabbie and passenger lasted the duration of our five-minute drive.

I paid with unfamiliar bills I'd drawn from the ATM at the airport, and we emerged at the front entrance of the behemoth store.

"So which is it—a bit of shopping first or fortify ourselves with some food?"

I could go for either, but from the way Louisa phrased the question I gathered she was ready for food. "Lunch, definitely," I said.

She led the way confidently through a huge department of luxury accessories, the kind where a single purse or briefcase occupies its own table or shelf, a way to make goods appear exclusive rather than to admit the cost of inventorying a large selection would be astronomical. Beyond, we walked into the world of food—cheeses, wines, meats, fruits and vegetables, and oh, the chocolate! I became distracted until I realized Louisa had gotten ahead of me.

She'd come to a stop at the entrance to an elegant room with tall pillars and intricate tile designs.

"Oh! My, this has changed." She didn't seem exactly happy. "Admittedly, it's been a couple of years since I've been in."

A jacketed maître d' approached. "Welcome to the new Dining Hall," he said with just the right amount of deference. "We've now many more offerings, something to suit every palate."

He pointed to a display of the menus, and we both exclaimed over dishes on the Pasta Bar's listing. He led us to that section. The hall was crowded and should have been noisy, but soft background music encouraged people to keep their voices low. Either that or everyone else was just as awestruck as I.

I ordered a fettucine dish with shrimp and a sauce I'd never heard of, while Louisa contented herself with a simple pasta decorated with sprigs of basil. With a glass of white wine apiece, we were soon sitting contentedly back in our chairs.

"To your arrival," Louisa said, raising her glass.

"To my hostess. And to a wonderful trip." Our meals arrived and I had to admit the creamy marsala sauce on my shrimp fettucine was amazing.

After finishing the meal by splitting an incredibly light tiramisu, we made our way upward via the escalator. I'd hoped to find a nice jacket for Drake, but everything was out of my budget, and although I found some gorgeous things in the ladies department, they were out of my league too. I passed on a $300 sweater and $500 slacks.

"But it's fun to browse," I told my aunt. "If I do any clothes shopping in England, it will have to be at places a commoner can afford."

She laughed. "Me too. I know just the places in Bury. They'll have some things that would be so cute on you. For now, though, I sense that your eyelids are drooping toward sleep."

It was true. I hadn't felt jetlagged at first, but the long night and day were catching up with me.

"What can we do to pass a little time? I want to stay upright until a somewhat reasonable bedtime," I told her. "Keeping in mind my normal bedtime at home is around nine."

"It will still be daylight at that hour, but I'm sure we can draw the curtains and get you a good night's rest. Meanwhile, I thought of one tourist spot that could be fun, given how fond you are of solving a mystery."

She had my interest.

Chapter 3

She introduced me to 'the tube' and I bought a three-day pass. We navigated our way through two stops and landed at Madame Tussaud's wax museum. Okay, where was the mystery?

Then she pointed out the street name on the corner—Baker Street—and I saw the addresses. One minute down the road and we were at 221B Baker Street, home of the world's most famous and enduring sleuth. Of course, fictional Sherlock never actually lived in this very real home, but apparently the books became so popular in their day that the residents were constantly being pestered by avid readers. So a special historical preservation group bought the residence and opened it for the curious.

I had to admit I wasn't exactly up on my Sherlockiana, having last read the stories when I was in high school, but this was great fun. Each room was furnished as per the stories, we were assured by the young docents who were stationed in each room, probably to be sure no one pilfered a pipe or hat or cape.

Costumes from the period represented characters in certain books, and I found myself thinking about the famed sleuth who used his powers of observation and extensive knowledge of trivial things in a time before the internet was a glimmer in anyone's eye. How lazy we've become, able to tap a few links on our phones and find out nearly anything we need to know.

In the gift shop I bought tins of tea for Elsa and Dottie and a large magnifying glass for Ron—not that he would actually use it, but he also refused to wear the reading glasses the optometrist had recently prescribed.

By the time Louisa and I had navigated the tube back to our hotel, I was feeling a definite energy lag. I took a hot shower and pulled on my nightshirt. I was in my bed moments later, assuring her if she wanted to keep the lights on for reading or to watch TV, nothing in the world would keep me awake.

* * *

The next two days flew by. London is a city of museums and shopping and flat-out wonderful experiences. Riding the double-decker red buses gave us a great chance to stop and visit all the places I'd ever heard of, and a trip over the top of the London Eye (don't call it a Ferris wheel!), on a perfectly clear day presented the ancient city beautifully.

By Sunday morning we were retrieving Louisa's small blue Ford from the public car park. She seemed a little shaky on some of the turns to get us out of the middle of the huge city, but once we hit the motorway northbound, it was an easy drive into Bury St. Edmunds.

The small town was every bit as quaint-charming-idyllic as I remembered, and I couldn't wait to get out and re-explore. We passed the Angel Hotel where I had stayed a couple of nights on my first visit. She made a turn and pulled to the curb on a street lined with shops.

"After a week of restaurant meals in the city, I'm leaning towards making dinner at home tonight," she said. "A Sunday roast sounds like just the ticket. If you don't mind a quick stop, I'll pop in to Marks and Spencer to pick up a few items. Won't take me two shakes."

I remembered the enticing array of foods in the department store, but there would be time to explore on my own later. If I trailed Louisa inside now, she'd never get dinner in the oven on time. I sat in the car and watched a young mother with two children walking toward the toy shop. The toddler clung to her mother's hand while the older child, a boy in short pants and a tidy pullover shirt, skipped ahead and pressed his hands to the glass. I couldn't see what was in the window display, but it certainly had his full attention.

Louisa was correct—she'd gone in and out of the store in under five minutes, emerging with a carrier bag containing a small cut of beef, white potatoes, carrots, and a package of frozen peas. I lost track of the exact turns she made along the two-lane streets, but we arrived at her brick row house in only a couple of minutes.

"There now. We'll just get the luggage from the boot," she said, looping the handles of the shopping bag over her arm. "You may settle into your room—you remember the one—top of the stairs, and I shall get this into the oven for our dinner. I must confess, I've never quite adapted to the English custom of dinner at eight. I suppose my American habits became too deeply ingrained. I normally eat at what the British consider teatime, around five. If that's all right with you?"

We'd had this conversation during the London days, too, but I didn't remind her. I merely agreed that an early dinner suited me fine and climbed the stairs with my big suitcase awkwardly in tow. My bedroom was exactly as I remembered it, with yellow floral wallpaper and bright royal blue accents. The closet and an empty dresser drawer had enough space for my clothes, which was all that mattered at the moment.

While the clinks and clatters of domestic kitchen noises went on downstairs, I took a moment to wash my face and check my hair—not that there's a lot you can do with a mop that's shoulder-length and straight. Except that when it's adapting to the English humidity, it has become somewhat bushy and only deserves to be wrapped up in a messy bun. The cool air reaching my neck felt good. That resolved, I figured I'd better offer some help in the kitchen.

Louisa was at the sink, washing her hands, then reaching for a towel.

"No, love, it's all taken care of for now. In two hours, we'll be ready. Shall we get a glass of wine and sit in the garden?"

"Who were the street performers we passed coming in? I think they were in the parking lot at the Angel?"

"Oh, yes. Another Sunday tradition here. There are all sorts of little groups. They practice endlessly. I tried joining one when I came here, but it can be somewhat clannish.

None wanted to take on a newcomer, and when I found a group who would give me a chance I found I was hopeless at memorizing the movements. Silly of me to even try. I was terrible at dance classes in school, too." She chuckled and raised her glass. "But here's to you. If you find a group to join while you're here, more power to you!"

"Oh, heavens. Not me. Besides, I doubt I'd fit anyone's idea of being part of a clan."

"Well, I probably used the word incorrectly. I doubt they're actually related. More like 'exclusive' in their choosing. One of the volunteers at the Tourism Office belongs to one of these groups. He's the drummer. Taps out the rhythm for the others to follow. He's quite proud of their reputation. They made the cut to go to a county-wide competition once."

She took another sip of her wine. "Of course, there were also tales of dissension and bickering within the group too. Count me out."

With a wink, she left her wine glass on the table and walked over to check something in her herb garden.

"During the weekdays I should really put in an appearance at my job, after being away this past week," she said with a laugh. "So you'll have some time free of your tiresome old auntie. But by evening we shall come up with someplace interesting to have dinner."

I protested that she was anything but tiresome; the days in London had been amazing and we'd covered a lot of ground. We finished our wine and went inside, where the perfectly done roast beef and fresh veggies turned out to be exactly right.

Chapter 4

I woke the next morning surprised to see by the bedside clock that it was already after ten o'clock. I thought of Drake, missed his voice, but this was not the hour to call home and wake anyone in the middle of the night. Plus, once he was awake, he would most likely need to be airborne on the job. He would call me when he had the chance.

I padded downstairs in my jammies and bare feet where I found a note on the kitchen table alongside a bag of scones, a jar of raspberry jam, and the crock of butter Louisa preferred to the type in a standard rectangular stick.

These are fresh from the bakery. But feel free to help yourself to anything at all. Have a beautiful day!

With love, L

I switched on the kettle and warmed one of the scones, having the idea to sit out in the garden to enjoy the light breakfast. I hadn't realized, until I pushed aside the curtain over the kitchen window, that a light drizzle was falling. The soft rain and grey sky were probably the reasons I'd slept so long and so well.

At home, when one doesn't have a job to go to, a rainy day is the perfect excuse to stay in and read a book or make a big pot of stew or something. But I realized the English dealt with far more wet weather than I'd ever see in my lifetime, and no one stayed indoors because of it. There was a stand full of umbrellas near the front door, and I could most certainly make good use of one of them.

After my little breakfast, I dressed in a couple of layers. The change in weather had put an end to the so-called heatwave, and although it was still summer I had no idea how chilly it might feel once I got out to the streets and walked for awhile. I wanted to see it all and do it all, remembering favorite shops. It would also be good to scout out the restaurant choices and study the menus posted outside, in case Louisa asked my preference for tonight's dinner.

Whatever we chose to do, it would be fun. I had the feeling I still hadn't heard a fraction of Louisa's fascinating adventure stories, and I got the idea that I should write them down to preserve them as the legacy of our most daring family member. I pondered that as I hitched my purse onto my shoulder and picked up one of the umbrellas.

I made my way toward Angel Lane, which led to the shops. The soft patter of raindrops on my little portable canopy provided a soothing backdrop and muffled the sounds of the cars that whooshed along the narrow roads.

Although I had loved every minute of our time in London, today it felt good to have a morning with no agenda.

From my previous visit, I remembered enough of the layout of the streets and locations of businesses that I had no trouble finding my way. And, other than bringing home a few gifts for those at home, there was no pressure to be any certain place. I stopped in at a cute bookshop, smaller than the Waterstones I'd been to before.

Two men stood behind the counter, fair-haired and gray versions of the same person. The older man greeted me, and the son barely looked up when I walked in. He handed a sheaf of cash register receipts to his father, muttered something, and shoved his arms into the sleeves of a blue blazer.

I'd spotted the umbrella stand at the door, left mine there, and held the door for the man who brushed past me. I made my way toward the fiction section. Having a book by a local author to read would be a real treat. I envisioned myself cuddling in and reading while Louisa was at work each day, a rarity for me at home.

I found the novel, a crime story by Ian Rankin—as if I didn't get enough of detectives, criminals and mayhem in real life. The book had been a bestseller and I could have bought a copy at home, but there was something about getting the British edition and reading it here that made the venture seem different.

Near the checkout desk stood a spinner of journals and planners. My earlier idea came back—this would be the perfect way to take notes about Louisa's tales. I supposed I should ask her about this plan. She might not want her life detailed in this manner. But I went ahead and chose a blank book with a beautiful cover, a hand-painted hummingbird on a backdrop of flowers, embellished with touches of sparkle and glitter. I tucked my purchases into my bag and opened the door.

"Don't forget your brolly," the bookstore guy called out.

"Thanks. Obviously, I'm not used to carrying one." I reached for the tan handle of the one I'd brought.

"We get quite the collection of spares here, over time." He turned back to his work, what I'd noticed looked like accounting sheets, profit and loss statements or something. Must have been engrossing reading—those few words were the most he'd uttered during our whole transaction.

Out on the street, the rain had dwindled to a faint mist. The stone buildings had a fresh, bright look now and the hanging baskets of brilliant flowers at every light post definitely seemed happy. I walked past shops I remembered from before—the cancer research charity shop and the Cornish pasty place, which was doing a booming business with the lunch crowd.

The scent of the little pastry pockets filled with meaty goodness called out to me, but since I'd finished breakfast only an hour ago, those would have to wait. I reminded myself I had another week to savor all the town's delights. For now, I would take advantage of the lull in the weather and do a stroll through the Abbey Gardens.

The massive stone Abbey Gate sheltered a dozen pigeons who were apparently trying to either scavenge crumbs or find a dry spot. Two of them fluttered away when I walked through the archway; the rest simply outwalked me, their little heads bobbing in rhythm. I fast-walked along the uncrowded pathways, beneath full leafy trees, toward the ancient ruins that dotted the grounds.

The stone constructions were once the original abbey, now mostly pillars and piles of rock that had withstood nearly fifteen-hundred years of wind, weather, wars, and children climbing on them.

Beyond the open grassy spaces and the ruins, a dirt path led to a narrow bridge spanning a little stream. I stood there a moment, watching a family of ducks, listening to distant traffic so faint the calls of birds overrode it. I pulled out my phone and sent Drake a picture and short message: **How's things? Wish you were here!** followed by a string of silly emoji hearts and smiles. He would read it when he woke up, then he'd laugh and know how much I missed him, mainly because those goofy things really aren't my style.

I left the bridge, retracing my steps until the path joined the lawns again. In the distance to my left were the roofs of the municipal buildings, police station, and the law courts. Ahead was the cathedral whose tall spires dominated the skyline from anywhere. I'd heard there was a rose garden and herb garden near it. I could wend my way back in that direction and probably find my way through the old graveyard, where the headstones always provided a fascinating read.

Unfortunately, my vision of a completely leisurely stroll turned into a mad dash when the sky let loose and rain came bucketing down. I skipped the circuitous route and headed straight for the gate and accompanying shelter of buildings.

My poor old umbrella did little more than keep my hair dry, and by the time I reached the shelter of the Abbey Gate, the legs of my jeans and my shoes were fairly well saturated. I spotted a tea shop on the corner near the Angel

Hotel and made my way there. It would be a good spot to dry off and have a little lunch before heading back to the house. With luck the rain would quit by then.

At the counter I ordered a pot of tea and a chicken salad sandwich.

"Take one of the tables near the fire," the proprietress told me, taking in my bedraggled look. "I'll bring your food."

While I waited I looked at my surroundings. The small shop accommodated only a half-dozen tables, mostly empty now, but the space was crowded with shelves of teapots, candles, tins of teas, and other kitchen gadgetry. The wall farthest from me was covered in heavy plastic sheeting and I could sense something going on behind it.

"I'm Alva Brody, the owner. Sorry, I must apologize for the construction," the woman told me when she arrived to set down my plate. "We're expanding, as you might have guessed. Our line of teas and gifts has increased in popularity. We're bursting at the seams."

A heavy sound came from behind the plastic. I could envision a sledge hammer hitting a wall.

"In summer we have a decent amount of seating outdoors, and it's not so crowded in here, but come winter time, I hope to have twice this many tables indoors with nice displays of the kitchen wares and a separate entrance for those who only want to shop. It's why we've taken over the space next door."

"It looks like a big remodeling job, for sure."

"You're American?"

I nodded. "From New Mexico."

"And what is it you do there? It's not a land of wild Indians and such, is it?"

"No, we all get along really well." I went on to tell a little about my home state and the fact I had an aunt here in Bury. "I have a hand in a couple of businesses at home, a partner with my brother in a private investigation firm, and I'm also licensed to fly helicopters so I help my husband in his business."

"Private investigator, huh?"

That's not usually the one most people notice first.

"I'll leave you to your meal." She nodded and went to wait on a young woman with two preschoolers who'd come in.

I took my time and was halfway through my sandwich, which was seasoned with an excellent curry, when another loud bang sounded from the construction area. A curse of unintelligible slang words rang out, and a young man came dashing between the sheets of plastic, his eyes wild and his mouth twitching.

Alva looked up from the till, where she was making change for someone who'd walked in to buy a pastry. Her eyes questioned the guy who, judging by his work clothes covered in a thick layer of plaster dust, was obviously part of the construction crew.

"Bertie? What—?"

"Call the police!" he said breathlessly.

Chapter 5

Alva's customer scooted out the front door as quickly as a woman of seventy can probably move.

"Bertie, what on earth?" Alva asked.

"It's a … a … dead person." He stared at her, his freckles standing out against a very pale face.

Alva shrank back.

"We'll be needin' the police," Bertie repeated. "Carl says so."

At that moment a man in his fifties came through the plastic-covered doorway. His clothing bore the same coating of white dust as Bertie's. His expression was grim but not panicky. I tried to make myself as unobtrusive as the proverbial mouse in the corner. This was real excitement in a small town.

"Carl—what's this?"

"Let me use the phone? Mine's out in my van."

She handed him the receiver of a phone that sat near the till, crossing her arms over her chest. He punched three numbers. "Is it the police?" he asked, not letting the operator go through the spiel about stating the nature of the emergency.

"Well, it's not as I'd call it an emergency, but we got a dead body at the Brody Tea Shop. Better be sendin' a constable or somebody to take a look."

Carl didn't seem the least bit flustered. I wasn't sure I'd ever seen anyone deal with a death in quite such a matter-of-fact manner. Bertie was pacing and dithering. Alva seemed agitated.

"Did you have to mention the name of my shop?" she asked Carl. "This sort of thing isn't good for business."

"How else was they to know where to send the constable?"

Her mouth formed a tight line. "All right, but don't you be telling the whole town." She turned on Bertie. "You either! Word about this gets out, I'll know you're the ones."

She looked toward the plastic divider. "Now what's this all about?" She started to walk toward the curtain and push through.

"Wait!" I spouted out. "It could be a crime scene."

All eyes turned toward me. *Uh-oh.* What happened to my mouse-in-the-corner strategy?

Carl squinted his eyes as he looked at me. "And who're you to be talkin'?"

"She's a private investigator from America," Alva helpfully provided.

I *knew* I shouldn't have included that information. "Well, only sort of. What do you think happened, Carl?"

He puffed up his chest a little.

"Well, couldn't see much. But what it is, when we broke through the wall where the old stairs used to be, I spotted some bits of clothing. Seemed *off*, you know."

"And I saw the bones." Bertie couldn't help himself. "It's a skeleton in there, it is."

Which explained Carl's lack of panic in calling the police. No medical emergency or freshly dead corpse. I thought about the ancient roots of the town and wondered how long a body might remain in a wall. To be completely decomposed, I supposed it could have been there anywhere from five years to five hundred.

The police arrived in a white car with flashing blue lights on top. The siren blipped to a stop when the two officers got out. Alva clearly knew them.

"George, Paul—must you leave those lights flashing? People will think there's been trouble here in my shop."

The older man looked at the younger, a silent okay. Paul slinked back outside and turned them off.

Alva turned to me with introductions. "DS George Redding and DC Paul Edwards, our local police detectives. Before that, they were friends of my family since they were both in short pants." She turned toward the men. "Her name's Charlie. She's American."

"Please stick around, miss," said DS Redding, clearing his throat and taking charge. "All right. What's happened here?"

Carl and Bertie both spoke at once, and the constable asked them to lead the way so he could see for himself. Behind the plastic curtain no voices were raised, no accusations made, so the whole thing began to dim in importance. Both constables snapped photos like mad.

Alva busied herself rearranging the scones and teacakes in her bakery cases. She'd been told to turn over her Closed sign, so there really wasn't much else to do. I was finishing my tea when a coroner's vehicle arrived.

Figuring it could start to get interesting, I pretended to sip, watching a gray-haired man carry a folded black body bag into the construction area. Someone pulled the plastic curtain back to allow room to maneuver and I got a pretty good view of the process.

The two cops and the two from the coroner's office took positions around the skeleton, which was still clad in what appeared to be jeans, a patterned yellow shirt, and a dark jacket. Perhaps navy blue, perhaps a blazer. The boots were a style I hadn't seen a man wear since my childhood. I was making mental notes as quickly as I could. The skull still had some hair and my impression was that it was either dark brown or black—again, hard to tell with the coating of plaster dust Carl and Bertie had dislodged.

"… in his late thirties, early forties," the coroner was saying to his colleague.

Carl and Bertie had been ordered to sit at one of Alva's tables. Bertie's wide eyes were trying to get glimpses of what was going on, but his seat near the shop's front windows didn't have nearly the vantage point mine did. Carl turned down a cup of tea—he was plainly put out that he couldn't get back to work more quickly. Apparently time was money in his business, too.

It took awhile, but finally the two from the coroner's office lifted the bones into the body bag, hefted it onto a gurney and wheeled it through the shop and out the door. The constables were gathering a few last bits of evidence when their radios began to squawk.

I missed the details, but got the gist when they hurriedly packed up their cardboard box of samples and rushed toward the door. A bad accident on the rain-slick motorway was pulling all law enforcement at the city and county levels to keep things under control.

DC Edwards handed Alva a business card, saying she should get in touch if she remembered anything that could help their investigation. He barely glanced toward me, so I took it to mean I was dismissed.

The construction workers seemed glad to get back to work, although I sensed Bertie really wished he'd been more involved in the investigation. No doubt he'd be the life of the party at the pub tonight.

I left my cozy fireside table and gathered my things. The rain had abated now. I texted to find out whether Louisa was still at work or had gone home. Home it was, so I headed in that direction. I hadn't thought to check my messages while I was warm and dry and comfortable, but I gave my phone a quick glance as I walked. Drake was fine, working long hours. Dottie assured me Elsa and Freckles were doing great. I sent each of them a thumbs-up and a smiley face.

Ron wanted to know if I'd done the month-end billing yet.

No—I'm on vacation. I texted that I would get it done tonight. Killjoy. I dropped my phone into my pocket and set a brisk pace to Louisa's house.

"How about tapas tonight?" she asked the moment I stepped in the door. "There's a wonderful place here, and I called ahead to see if the flamenco guitarist is playing this evening. He is. *And* they make the best sangria!"

It sounded like an offer I couldn't refuse. And if the

sangria was super good, Ron's customers might not receive their billing until tomorrow. Too bad.

No rain was forecast for the evening but we carried our umbrellas anyway, walking the few blocks to the restaurant. I didn't know how I had missed this one—it was just down the street from several of the shops where I'd been today, including the Brody Tea Shop.

I mentioned the afternoon's excitement to my aunt.

"That must have been a bit weird for you," she said. "Brody Tea Shop … I don't think I've ever been there. Would have thought I'd eaten at every single place in this little town, wouldn't you?"

We arrived at La Fontana at that moment and she steered me inside where, no surprise, she greeted the couple who owned the place like old friends.

"I've known Carlos and Maria since before I moved to Bury. We were practically neighbors for a while."

The couple were in their seventies, and I quickly learned that the restaurant was a family enterprise. A woman in her fifties was the hostess, kept busy by seating new arrivals.

"All the waitstaff are either grandchildren or nieces and nephews," Louisa told me as we took seats at a narrow table. "And the chef and most of his kitchen helpers are Maria's children. There's already a great-grandchild coming into the business, that little girl who is filling water glasses."

She flipped her napkin onto her lap and ordered a pitcher of the sangria. "Wait until you hear the guitarist. He's another of Carlos' and Maria's sons."

"It takes a big family to operate a restaurant this size," I commented. "You've known them a very long time?"

"Since Spain. I was at their wedding. In fact, a few years later, they were the ones who told me they were moving to

England and told me about discovering this town."

Wow. Small world. The sangria arrived and she poured each of us a glass. She was *so* right about how wonderful it tasted.

"Have you ever told me what you did in Spain—what took you there?"

"Oh, gosh. A man. A relationship that didn't last too long, but that was followed by my taking classes at the flamenco institute, meeting another man ... maybe another after that." She laughed and looked at me with bright eyes. "You have to understand, it was the freewheeling '80s, right before AIDS became a scare. And a lot of Europe didn't have the uptight, stuffy attitudes that were prevalent in America. We were all just out to have a good time."

"You danced flamenco?"

A coy look from under her lashes. "I did. I could still do it today."

Surprise must have registered on my face.

"Unlike a lot of trendy dances, flamenco embraces dancers and players of all ages, and it's a family activity. It's not uncommon to see grandmothers dancing with their toddler grandchildren while their sons play instruments and daughters keep time with the *palmas*." She demonstrated the quiet, rhythmic clapping of the hands. "There are many distinct rhythms in flamenco. Most of us are lucky to differentiate two or three, but the gypsies, the flamenco community ... they'll know the moment you're off the beat."

A young woman who looked barely out of her teens showed up beside our table, balancing a tray with an assortment of food. No one had asked for our order, so I guessed this was Louisa's favorite or she had transmitted some kind of secret menu request. The various plates and small dishes were filled with traditional Spanish tapas—olives, tiny potatoes, slices of hard cheese and serrano ham, interesting sauces—and everything was presented beautifully.

At some point the recorded music from hidden speakers around the room faded out and a man took his seat on the raised platform that stood a step higher than the rest of the room. He gave an intricate riff with his fingertips across the guitar strings before launching into a very complicated piece. There was no sheet music on the stage with him, only his concentration on the instrument and the notes.

"It's called a *Zapateado*," Louisa whispered. "The piece is over nine minutes long. It's not one of the traditional rhythms for dancing, but a standalone piece written by Paco de Lucía."

How did she know all this stuff? I realized my aunt's life was far more diverse and complex than I'd ever imagined. How sad that my father and grandfather had tried to quash her enthusiasms and fit her into their mold. It was the reason for the rift that had kept Louisa out of our lives so long.

We nibbled, taking our time and enjoying the music and wine. At one point the girl who'd been our waitress appeared on the small stage next to the guitarist. She now wore a red dress with layers of ruffles on the long skirt. Another young man, whom I'd seen behind the bar, set up a square box and sat upon it. He started a pattern of beats by tapping on the front of the box drum between his legs. The guitarist picked up the rhythm and the girl began the dance. I found myself completely enthralled. Growing up in an area with heavy Spanish influence, I was surprised I'd never explored this. And now, in a very small town in southeast England, I was learning about it from my world-traveler aunt.

Afterward, we walked home, mellowed by sangria, intensified by the music and dance. It was only as we passed the Brody Tea Shop that I again remembered the discovery of the afternoon. Someone's life would be changed when they learned of this unknown victim. The thought sobered me, and I vowed to look up the case and find out what had happened to the poor abandoned man behind the wall.

Chapter 6

Louisa was up first in the morning. I could hear her in the kitchen below, humming bits of Spanish-sounding songs, her feet tapping every now and then on the old linoleum floor. I smiled.

"I'm off to work this morning," she announced cheerily when I walked in.

I had put on jeans and a lightweight sweater, and I'd managed to run a brush through my hair, but I felt nowhere near as chipper as she appeared.

"My hangover cure," she said, handing me a glass of something that looked like juice. "Don't ask, just drink it down."

It tasted somewhere between salty and fruity, and almost immediately the dull feeling in my head went away. "What—?"

"A little recipe I learned many years ago." She picked up a small thermal bag. "All right then, I'm off. Enjoy your day."

She sent a little air kiss in my direction as she breezed out of the kitchen. I heard the front door open and close. I looked around and found cereal and fresh fruit. A small TV set on a corner shelf was tuned to the morning news show, a format so similar to those in the US that I would have sworn I was home except for the precise accents of the anchor team.

While I munched my cereal, I found myself caught up in the local news stories—also very similar to home, with emphasis on accidents and crimes. I listened with one ear, briefly wondering whether the discovery of the body in the wall here in Bury would come up. It didn't. Instead, it seemed the big accident on the motorway was the top story, complete with warnings to drivers about the way roads will become more slippery during a heavy rain.

I turned my attention to my computer, which I'd carried down with me. Ron's reminder was still out there; I hadn't done the monthly billing and for some reason he would expect the company to continue making money whether I was out of the country or not. While the laptop booted up, I washed the dishes and set them to dry. Louisa's quaint 1950s kitchen didn't include a dishwasher, so this was my bit toward helping domestically.

The television news continued to drone on, interspersed with witty repartee from the morning show hosts and plenty of bashing of the way Parliament handled things. Pretty much like home.

I got into my accounting program and updated the customer payments, got a report of who owed what, and generated statements to be emailed to each of them. That should keep my nagging brother happy.

A banner at the bottom of the TV screen caught my eye when I reached for my mug. Gruesome Murder in Suffolk County. My first thought went to yesterday's discovery of the body at the tea shop, but this was in another town and involved a high society woman. Plus, the old skeleton had not exactly been gruesome, or necessarily a murder. The man could have fallen down the abandoned stairwell.

Right. And no one noticed when the section was walled in? Didn't seem too likely but it was a possibility I needed to consider.

Look at me, talking like I have a case to solve.

What if I do? I mean, I can only spend so much time shopping and eating.

My duties back home had been quickly dispatched, and the hours of the day stretched ahead while Louisa was at work. My silly mind began to race.

Clearly, the police were distracted now by the new murder, one in which they might actually have a chance of catching the killer. But there might be another killer at large, one who believed he'd gotten away with murder.

Charlie, Charlie, Charlie … watch out. You're in a foreign country and there's no Kent Taylor-type buddy in the police department to get you out of a scrape.

I needed a plan. Step 1 – Find out the identity of the victim. Step 2 – Find out the cause of death.

Beyond that, the trail could go anywhere. Most likely there was a cold case file at the local station. Somebody who went missing a long time ago and it's discovered he died accidentally. Case closed, all wrapped up.

Before I even let the word *murder* into my head, I needed to know the basics. I left my computer on the kitchen table, picked up my purse and headed out. The rain had moved out during the night and a lovely, sunny day was promised by that little weather app on my phone. I set off toward the center of town.

Since I was passing it anyway, I decided my first stop would be Alva Brody's tea shop. Heck, she might have had another visit from the police, who clarified everything. In that case I'd need to find something else to do for the day.

Alva was wiping crumbs from one of the tables in the shop. Behind the plastic construction divider I could hear voices and hammering, so it seemed Carl and Bertie were on the job again. I stood at the pastry display case, scoping out the offerings. As a nice gesture I could at least take home something for tonight's dessert, especially since I intended to quiz Alva relentlessly.

Unfortunately, there was no 'relentless' about it. When I asked whether she'd been told anything more about yesterday's events, she simply shrugged and said no.

"It's not as if the police confide in the likes of me," she said as she circled around behind the bakery case. "I read through the paper this morning. Didn't see anything there either."

I hadn't thought about a newspaper. Shows how far certain habits have slipped from my routine. At least now I needn't bother. Alva made it sound as if she'd looked it over pretty carefully. I bought a beautiful fruit tart and asked if she could hold onto it for me while I did another errand.

A brisk fifteen minute walk took me to the police station, a squarish building of tan bricks with a crisp blue and white sign at the door. Inside, the public reception area was fairly quiet. I inquired of the female sergeant at the desk.

"Who would I speak to about skeletal remains that

were discovered yesterday?"

A cool blue glance came my way. The woman picked up the phone and spoke quickly to someone. Edwards, the younger of the two detectives who'd been at the scene yesterday, came walking out through a heavy door that led to the back of the building. He gave me the kind of curious look that didn't indicate whether he remembered me or not. But he was kind enough to take me to a desk and offer me a chair.

"I was just talking with Alva Brody," I said. "She seems very concerned about the body that was found yesterday." Both of those statements were absolutely true, although they implied a closeness between myself and Mrs. Brody that didn't actually exist. "Has your department located a missing person's case that matches? I mean, in order to find out the man's identity?"

"I … I'm not actually certain," he said, his eyes darting over the piles of paper on his desk. "It's been a little hectic here today. Most of our team are at a new crime scene."

"I heard." I spotted a bold black heading on one of the pages near his left hand. Office of the Coroner it said at the top, although the rest of it was covered by some other sheets. Apparently, the man simply dropped all his filing in the middle of the desk. As I watched, his hand managed to shift several pages and cover up the small bit I could see.

"I'm meant to be joining them, Miss …"

"Parker. Charlie." I eyed the messy papers. "What about the coroner's report? If it's arrived, maybe you've learned the cause of the victim's death?"

"Actually, we have procedures. We'll be processing the information and checking our own files before we can release any of that to the public."

Someone stepped into the doorway and called his name just then. As he stood to respond, his hand shifted the papers, and I could once again see the heading. Since reading upside down is a skill I've perfected over the years, I also saw that the autopsy had been performed on an "unknown white male."

Edwards stood and turned to get something the other person was requesting, a plastic bag with red Evidence tape across it. I was sorely tempted to slip the coroner's report closer to myself to get a really good look, but that would surely be noticed. I settled for memorizing the phone number for the coroner's office, located for my convenience at the top of the page.

Chanting the number in my head, I thanked DC Edwards and wished him a nice day. Outside his cubicle I found a scrap of paper in my purse and jotted it down. Then I hurried out of the building and retraced my steps back toward the gardens. At last I felt I was on the way to learning something.

A bench in the shade beckoned and I pulled out my cell phone. Even if the office had caller ID, I had a plausible excuse all worked out.

"Office of the county coroner," said a polite voice.

"Hello, yes. I'm an American college student here on a summer internship at the police department. My supervisor has asked me to follow up and see if a certain autopsy report is ready. It's for a John Doe set of skeletal remains recovered at a shop in downtown Bury St. Edmunds yesterday."

I got transferred to a harried-sounding male, who informed me the report had been sent to the police this morning. But when I pretended to search for a moment and informed him that I couldn't find it anywhere, he allowed as how he could make a copy and I could drop by to pick it up. My ignorance as a young student and an American was all the excuse I needed to get the address.

Thirty minutes later I walked out with my very own copy of the report. Granted, I'd had to sign for it, and I knew I was treading close to something not quite legal—probably. Although I justified it with a bunch of my own ideas—the report was probably going to become public record anyway at some point; the police were too busy to work this case right now; it wasn't as if this neglected set of bones had scads of people trying to identify it.

If I were home in Albuquerque, I might try some or all of those excuses on Kent Taylor, the homicide detective I had crossed paths with a number of times. Here in another country … well, I'd better just keep my head low until I had some information that would be so incredibly helpful they couldn't possibly be angry over my little infraction.

To make myself feel better, I stopped at the Cornish Pasty shop and got one to take home.

Chapter 7

ack at Louisa's kitchen table—which was beginning to look like an impromptu desk with my computer and the assortment of papers I'd begun to collect—I nibbled at my chicken and mushroom lunch while I studied the coroner's report.

I skimmed over what I knew already—unknown white male in his late 30s or early 40s—and skipped to the cause of death. Blunt trauma to the head. That was it. No other injuries were described. The condition of the skeleton suggested the man had been dead for more than twenty years. In the conclusion section at the bottom, the coroner had suggested "possible death by misadventure." I had to look up the word. *An accident or unintended result of a person's own actions.*

So, the pompous guy who'd handed me the report

might have been right when he speculated that the unknown young man had simply fallen down the stone steps and hit his head. If he wasn't dead immediately, perhaps he was so stunned and disoriented that he couldn't get himself out before he died there.

Still, there was the fact that the wall had been closed in around this old stairwell. No one noticed a body? No one noticed the smell? It would have had to be seriously bad in there for quite awhile. An accidental cause just didn't sit well with me. I wondered if the police had thought the same thing, but Edwards' demeanor this morning didn't indicate he was all that concerned over this one.

I drummed my fingers on the tabletop, pondering. I really couldn't go barging back in at the police station, asking what other forensic evidence they'd collected, asking to see their crime scene photos. Too bad I was not really a college intern with access to the files in the station. This was their case and I would have to leave the detecting to them.

I pictured how it would go—a file created, drifting to the bottom of the stack as more urgent cases came in, eventually going into a deep basement room in a cabinet labeled Cold Cases. Face it, the poor body was already pretty cold.

Maybe Ron would have some ideas for me. A look at the clock told me it was still way too early in the morning to call New Mexico. What would my brother be able to say, anyway? My mind ran through a few possible scenarios, none of them ending in the answers I wanted. Kent Taylor would be no help. Odds were he'd had a couple of fresh murders of his own to solve overnight.

Our receptionist's face popped into my head. Awhile

back Sally had mentioned something a friend of hers was doing online. There was a group of amateur sleuths who looked into cold cases the police had worked but abandoned, and they'd actually had a few successes. *Now what was the name?*

My computer mocked me, sitting there with the lid closed. Dummy Charlie—just Google it. More than a few such organizations popped up. Interesting. I had to narrow down my search terms or I could be at this all week. I tried adding *missing person* and *Bury St. Edmunds, UK*, but no simple answer dropped in my lap.

Okay, *missing person, male*, and a date range that would include what I'd learned from the autopsy. There were hundreds of cases in the US alone. But one group's name stood out. They investigated crimes worldwide, not only in America, and the name Sleuths International seemed familiar. If it was the one Sally's friend belonged to, I might gain some insider help. I went to their site, signed up for a basic user account and ignored their plea for a donation to help offset costs. That could come later, if I actually found anything of use.

The first thing I noticed was that every case had a photo. Of course. Someone who reported a loved one missing always gave the police a photo to work from. My problem was that I had no idea what my victim had looked like, other than the tuft of dark hair I'd seen. The site wasn't exactly designed for the type of hunt I was trying to do. Most people trying to find out information on a missing person would begin with the victim's name and go from there.

I began by narrowing the search to males who had last been seen in the UK. Reason told me someone wouldn't likely transport a body from another country all the way to this tiny town just to stash it in a stairwell. I also eliminated children and young teens. This victim had been older. Even so, my search still netted more than a hundred names during the time in which our guy likely was here.

Scanning the profiles one by one was the only method left once I had the list. I quickly skimmed the photos and eliminated blonds and redheads. Most guys don't color their hair. I also knew it wasn't someone of African or Asian descent, based on what the coroner's report said. Plus, the report gave the victim's height. That was handy. The list of a hundred dwindled gradually to about two dozen.

The light in the room had changed subtly but I hadn't noticed it until I heard Louisa's cheery voice from the front parlor. Had the entire day slipped by me?

"Hello, my busy girl," she greeted. "Hard at work? That brother of yours is a regular taskmaster, isn't he?"

"Oh, I finished his stuff way early. I've got myself wrapped up in a local mystery."

"Well, I've scored us a nice little change of pace," she announced, reaching into the pocket of her skirt. "Tickets to a play at the Apex. One of the actors came around the office today, asking us to attend so we could recommend it for the rest of their summer run here in Bury."

I reluctantly closed the lid on my laptop.

"Oh, don't be such a workaholic. A break will do you good—will do us both good. It's *One Man, Two Guvnors*, and it's the theatre group from Cambridge putting it on, so I know it will be wonderful."

She was right. My head felt stuffy and too full of facts and data. A break would serve to clear the cobwebs and give me clearer insights in the morning. I hoped. While Louisa went upstairs to change clothes and freshen up, I bookmarked a few pages.

The play was good, but I found myself mentally drifting and then snapping to attention to figure out what I'd missed. I did manage to laugh at all the right places and Louisa seemed convinced, when we drifted into a pub for a late supper afterward, that I'd been present all along.

By the time we walked home and settled into our rooms, I felt recharged enough to resume my computer search. I'd carried my laptop up with me and sat in bed with it across my knees. My handwritten list of the names I considered possibilities lay beside me on the cheery yellow duvet. I'd also made a quick checklist of the characteristics of the skeleton from the coroner's report: Height – 6'1", Age – late 30s to early 40s, Black hair. Most likely a slender build. I wondered how they knew that, since the flesh was long gone, and then abandoned that train of thought due to the *ew* factor.

It was slightly past midnight when I came upon one profile that matched everything. Reported missing when he was thirty-nine years old, an American from Alabama whose sister, Caroline, said he led a vagabonding lifestyle, hitting the road and going wherever a whim took him. It was long before mobile phones were common. No texting or social media back then, but they'd made a pact. Out of respect for their parents, he had agreed to check in by calling home every week, although Caroline admitted she was actually lucky to hear from him once or twice a month. She'd last heard from him in London, where he'd talked about the music scene and sitting in as drummer with a band. She even added the side remark that he wasn't a very good musician but liked the lifestyle and found gigs now and then.

She finally reported him missing when she hadn't

heard from him in six months. Why so long? They were not a close family, but their elderly mother wanted to know everyone was all right. When their mother passed away, Caroline had kept up the habit, even though she was busy with a husband and children of her own.

I scrolled back to the top of the page, where a high school kid gave a lopsided, Elvis-like grin. The type of face that would probably become sexier and even more appealing as he aged. A few other photos had been added, casual poses in black leather and denim, some with motorcycles, one with a guitar strap slung over his shoulder. He looked like a wanderer even then.

His name was Mark Cardrick. I captured a couple of the better photos with my phone.

Chapter 8

Although my thoughts were buzzing with this new information about the body in the wall, my eyelids were threatening to slam shut. I slept fitfully, with the pictures of Mark Cardrick drifting in and out of my consciousness. When I did finally settle into sound sleep, it was to wake well after midmorning. Louisa had left a note on the kitchen table: *Today's my early afternoon off. Shall we have high tea at the Angel? I'll get a booking.*

Although I was already feeling fairly obsessed with finding answers to what I was beginning to think of as my new case, I really was here to visit my aunt and our times together were always fun. It wasn't as if a mad murderer was on the loose, making time of the essence in solving this one.

I poured cereal and milk in a bowl and set up my

laptop and a growing number of notes on the kitchen table. First thing, I went back to Sleuths International and paid the extra fifty dollars for a premium membership, which promised in-depth access to any available police files and contact information for those interested parties who had agreed. I assumed this meant relatives of the missing person. Who else, after all these years, would be interested?

Sure enough, a treasure trove of information popped up when I gave my new passcode, including some on Mark Cardrick's sister who had filed the original missing-person report. Caroline Cardrick Baker lived in Mobile, Alabama, at the time. There was an address and phone number. I would wait until a decent hour and phone.

But wait. There were notes in a different font, indicating these were additions to the file by someone in the Sleuths community. **Caroline Baker passed away 2/17/91**. Approximately a year after she'd filed the report. I felt a sense of letdown. Had she been ill and wanted to locate her brother before it was too late?

My phone rang, startling me. Louisa.

"I was able to get us a booking for tea at the Angel Hotel," she said. "Four o'clock. It's a substantial enough spread we most likely won't want dinner afterward. And don't get terribly full on lunch either."

I laughed. "Sounds like fun. Is this a dress-up thing?"

"Not really. No hats or gloves required. A pretty dress will do." She said she would meet me in the lobby, then clicked off the call.

A pretty dress. Ooh. Being a girl generally given to wearing jeans and T-shirts, I couldn't immediately think of a single pretty dress I owned. Well, other than a truly glamorous holiday gown my sister-in-law had given me a few Christmases ago. I dashed upstairs to check out my wardrobe options.

It turned out I had packed a skirt and matching summery top. It would be fine. As for the possibility of coming up with a hat or gloves … that was never happening in my lifetime. Good thing it wasn't a requirement. I laid out the outfit and budgeted time enough for a shower and shampoo beforehand.

Back at my desk, I continued to peruse the Cardrick page on Sleuths International. Another phone number had been noted in the alternate font, shortly after the notation about Mark's sister having died. By the surname I guessed it belonged to one of her sons.

It was still early in the US, but I could try. I tapped in the international dialing code and number. My phone bill was going to be horrendous this month.

A sleepy male voice answered. I said I was calling from England and used the excuse that I'd wanted to catch him before he left for work.

"Who is this?" he muttered.

"I'm part of a team working to solve the case of your uncle who was reported missing a long time ago." It sounded better than saying I was a nosy person who couldn't resist a mystery.

"You got the wrong person, lady. I ain't got an uncle."

"Wait—are you related to Caroline Cardrick Baker?"

His sleepy tone vanished. "My mother. She died a long time ago."

"Yes, I recently learned that. But before it happened, she had reported her brother, a Mark Cardrick, missing. The last she heard from him he was in London."

There was a soft groan, and I pictured him sitting up in

bed after being so rudely awakened by me. "I don't know nothing about that. We're pretty close with Daddy's family, but Mama's never did come around much. None of us ever really knew them, and I'm pretty sure I never even met any uncle named Mark."

"Okay, thanks. I was hoping maybe he'd been in touch after your mother passed, that he might have even come back to be nearer to the family."

"Not that I know of."

"Can you take my number? In case any of your other relatives would know?"

"And why are you doing this?"

I took a deep breath. "Mainly to find out if the Mark Cardrick reported missing in 1990 is still alive. There's been a body found here, in England. It could be him, and I'm sorry to tell you this over the phone. But if he came back home, it's a good possibility the person here isn't him."

"Yeah, well. I can ask around but I'd be surprised if anybody's been in touch with him here. Like I said, my daddy's family we've kept up with. Not the Cardricks at all, as far as I know."

I thanked him and apologized for calling so early. There basically wasn't anything else I could do. If other clues pointed to the John Doe actually being this Cardrick dude, the police could at least contact these American relatives for DNA samples for matching. But that seemed a way off in the future, at this point.

I washed my cereal bowl and did a few stretches to work the kinks out of my back. So far, I'd only managed to get brushed off by the police and to piss off a poor man in Alabama whom I'd awakened way too early.

Still, now that I had the name of Mark Cardrick, I

could do some more internet browsing. There were a few Cardricks on Facebook and Instagram, but without friending and following for awhile, I couldn't see the point. What would I learn, really? And it felt a little like stalking to watch someone's account in hopes they would slip up and mention a long-lost cousin or uncle or boyfriend. Face it, Mark had disappeared before the internet or social media were a *thing*.

I got impatient with the whole process and my shoulder was aching from so much time at the computer. I decided to take a brisk walk in anticipation of all the calories I would probably consume at teatime. I slung my purse strap over my shoulder and set out, circling several blocks of residential neighborhood, coming out near the Green King Brewery, and back by way of Westgate Street and past the Guildhall.

After all that I felt a little turned around but recognized a house with a bright red door, which I'd used in the past as a reference point for the turn to Louisa's street. Soon I was back in her cozy house, and it was time that I get busy with my shower and dressing for the big occasion.

Since my previous stay the hotel dining room had been redecorated with blue velveteen banquettes and modern art on the walls. High tea at the Angel included some of everything, as my aunt had promised. A three-tiered serving plate with a layer of savory baked treats, a layer of small sandwiches, and a layer of scones and sweet cakes. The selection of teas was out of my area of expertise so I let Louisa choose. The Darjeeling was excellent, by the way, and she was in high spirits as she told me about her upcoming tour next week of the town's haunted sites.

"Of course my favorite is the one I do at Halloween,"

she said, reminding me it had been that time of year at my last visit. "I add a few bits of witchy accessories to my ensemble and it's always a hit with the visitors."

It was nearly six o'clock when we pried ourselves from our seats and left the hotel.

"This was nice," I told her. "I'm so glad you thought of it."

"But I'd intended for it to be my treat." We'd gone through that ritual little tussle over the bill, and I had won by insisting afternoon tea was small compensation for my accommodations at her home.

Out on Abbeygate Street people were bustling in one direction for the most part, leaving the shopping district and heading for their cars and homes. We moved against the tide, pausing now and then for women with strollers or older couples who walked arm-in-arm. At the corner of High Baxter, I spotted two familiar faces.

Bertie spotted me first and waved. "Miss," he said, touching the brim of his cap.

"How are you? How's the project coming along?"

Carl dropped a large toolbox into the back of his van and turned toward me. "Well enough. Still a few weeks from completion."

"I imagine Alva would like the new space finished sooner?" I guessed.

Bertie gave a wry grin but didn't confirm my guess.

I turned to ask Louisa if she knew the two workers, to make introductions if necessary, but she had stepped back and was staring at the upper floors of the building. The men climbed into their vehicle and the engine started. Bertie's arm waved out the side window as they pulled away.

When I turned, Louisa was walking already, her gaze

on the paving stones, her face a little paler than normal. I caught up.

"Are you feeling all right?" I asked. "I hope something on the tea tray didn't disagree."

In a flash she brightened. "Oh no, I'm just fine."

But she still had that faded look.

She caught me scrutinizing her. "It looks as though you're finding some new friends locally."

"The workmen? Just friendly enough for a quick hello is about all. They discovered the body in the wall in that shop, so I guess we have the kinship of that."

She nodded and didn't say more. In fact, she didn't say much at all when we reached the house, changed out of our dresses and into comfy sweats, and met back in the living room to decide on our evening's entertainment.

"Is something wrong?" I finally asked. "You haven't been your usual bubbly self. Did something happen on the way home?" She'd been perfectly talkative during tea.

She sighed. "Nothing really. When you paused to talk to those men … It seemed there was a lot of spirit movement in the area or something."

I knew she felt psychic oddities more than most of us, but today? More so than normal?

Louisa switched the TV to a comedy show and I left my questions alone. She clearly wasn't in the mood to talk about whatever this was.

Chapter 9

The moment I picked up my phone the next morning it pinged with a new message. One of the privileges of my premium membership was direct contact with others in the sleuthing group. Someone from the Sleuths International site had noted my inquiry about Mark Cardrick's case.

There's more info on the case than appears on our site. Reply if interested.

Of course I was interested! I zipped a reply out to coldcasehannah before I even brushed my teeth. By the time I finished in the bathroom I'd received two messages from home—Ron and Drake—so I quickly responded to them, then went down to the kitchen for my first cup of coffee.

An hour passed, during which I glanced at my phone

screen about every thirty seconds. During that time I nearly panicked when I saw a message from Dottie Flowers, but began breathing again when I realized it had been sent the afternoon before. She just wanted to let me know Freckles was having a great time at their house and might be getting just the tiniest bit spoiled, as Elsa had insisted on buying the jumbo size bag of meaty treats. I shook my head a little but responded with two smiley faces.

Ron's message had asked for the combination to the office safe. I swear, the man can't remember anything. And Drake just sent a sad face followed by a string of hearts.

I'd finished two slices of toast and was midway through my second mug of coffee when a ping alerted me to something from coldcasehannah.

Link to extra page attached. Interesting case. If you are in Suffolk County, we could meet.

I wasn't so sure about a meeting. Online, a complete creep can call himself Hannah. I would bide my time.

I tapped the link and found an entire webpage devoted to the Cardrick case. The basic information on the case, shown to any casual browser, said Cardrick had last been seen in London. This page had actual copies of the police reports and the first thing that caught my eye was the trail had led to Bury St. Edmunds.

The next thing—and this one caused me to slosh my coffee—was one of those interviewed was a Louisa Parker.

Oh crap! If the police on the case today really began digging, how long would it take them to come back to her?

My guess—not long.

Not long *enough*.

A close relative needs your help. The prediction came back to me.

I grabbed my purse and headed toward the tourism office. I needed to have a word with Louisa.

* * *

"Of course I knew Mark," she said, trying for a matter-of-fact tone and not quite pulling it off. "And I would have told you this if you'd mentioned your interest."

We'd left her office and headed for the Abbey Gardens just down the road, so at least there was a degree of privacy for this conversation.

"I told you about the body. You never said a thing."

"Because … you didn't know the victim's name."

Hadn't I told her that part, once I discovered it? Maybe not. The few hours we'd spent together had been filled with other activities, and I'd been treating this case as more of a curiosity.

"Tell me more. He was an American …"

"Yes he was, with a charming Southern-boy accent." Her eyes went dreamy for a moment. "Although I noticed he could turn the Southern charm on and off as needed."

"Let's start at the beginning. When and where did you meet him?"

"Oh. Well, that was in Spain. We had a good time, lots of laughs. He introduced me to sangria—made the proper way. Oh my. In Cordoba, we sneaked a flask into the Mezquita and got more than slightly tipsy behind the choir seats in the chapel area. A docent, or whatever they're called back there, heard us giggling and we ran off. Oh, those red and white stripes—the arches and ceilings began to tilt and I nearly— Oh, but that wasn't as funny as the time in Sevilla—"

I grabbed her wrist and stopped walking. "Louisa! Focus."

Her smile faded.

"I'd love to hear all the stories. I really would. But I need to get to the facts kind of quickly." *Before the police do.* "So you met in Spain, traveled some … together? And then, after Spain? Were you still together when you came to England?"

She resumed walking, following the circular path that was flanked by neat plantings of bright petunias, geraniums, and delphinium.

"Let me think. From Barcelona, he said he had some business in Rome and asked if I wanted to go along. But I'd just been to Rome a few weeks before that. Plus, I suddenly had this desire to go to Morocco—if one is in southern Spain anyway, it's just right there … So we parted ways, said we would keep in touch. And I'm glad I went. Morocco just had something so …"

"Mark Cardrick," I interrupted. "Was that the last you saw of him?"

"Oh, no." We strode past the last of the benches and out to open lawns. I thought maybe she meant to leave the statement hanging, make me pry out the information a scrap at a time, but then she spoke again.

"It was Calais. I'd enjoyed all of Morocco I needed seriously, a couple of weeks is more than enough—and had made my way back through Spain and France. I was purchasing my ticket for the crossing to Dover. And there he was, waiting to get on the same ferry. 'It's been too long, Louisa,' is what he said. I believe it had actually been no more than two or three months since Barcelona. He was the first to call me *Louisa* with sort of a Spanish/Italian lilt. I liked it."

I took a breath. "So you came to England together?"

"I suppose, technically. As far as London, then we drifted again. I went to Cambridge in search of some interesting information in one of the university libraries, and one day I took a quick trip by train here to Bury. This was the town, of all I'd seen in the UK and Europe, that captured my heart."

"And Mark, during this time?"

"Oh, off on another adventure, I assumed. He was like that. Something or someone would catch his attention and off he'd go."

"He ended up here in Bury as well."

"Ah, yes." She pointed to a robin that had landed atop one of the ancient stone walls.

I was about to chew my knuckles. "With you? It's a small town. Did you see Mark here?"

"Well, of course I did. We lived together."

Lived together. At what point would she have thought to include this as an important fact? I forced my voice to be calm and patient.

"He lived with you … was it a long time or more like a quick stayover?"

"Oh, Charlie, I don't recall exactly. Probably a couple of months." She picked up a stray leaf from the ground and began picking it to small bits. "We, um, had words. I discovered some things about him I didn't much care for and I asked him to leave. The next day he was gone and never came back. I must admit, I somewhat hoped he would have a reasonable explanation and would apologize, but that didn't happen."

"You had words … over what? Something serious?"

"Oh, you know … typical man and woman stuff. He'd lied to me."

I sensed I wasn't going to get anything more specific, at least for now. "Think carefully. When was this? Do you recall the month and year? Or the season?"

"Not offhand, but I can probably figure—" Her phone rang out with the sound of a witch's cackle, startling us both. She fished down in the deep pocket of her skirt and pulled it out. "Uh-oh, my boss. I suppose I'd better head back."

She started walking toward the Abbey Gate before she'd finished the sentence. I started to trail along but decided—why? I needed to put my thoughts together with all the new information and see if I could piece together the story. So far, the fact Louisa and Mark had argued right before he vanished didn't seem like a good thing. Not a fact I'd want the police to dig out.

I caught up and gave her a hug, saying I would pick up something at the grocery for tonight's dinner so we could eat at home. I needed to get her in a quiet spot and try to get her to concentrate on this subject long enough to fill in the facts for me. Out in public places, around other people, she was simply too scattered.

It was on my way, so I stopped in again at Brody's Tea Shop. Alva was wiping down one of the small tables. The cheery fire had died to embers. Since it was a warm day, I assumed she only lit it in the early morning to take the chill off the room. Behind the plastic work-zone barrier, it was quiet. She looked up from her work and smiled, recognizing me.

"How's the construction coming along?" I asked after ordering a small loaf cake to take home for tonight's dessert.

"Ah. Slow." She glanced toward the silent area. "Carl's made some excuse about there being a stonemason's meeting this afternoon, or some such. Personally, I think he's got two jobs going and he's stretching himself too thin to do it all."

I nodded. "Have the police come back? I mean, investigating any more about that body?"

"No sign of 'em. Fine by me. Not good for my shop, that sort of nasty business going on." She wrapped the tea cake in paper and set it into a little box.

"I wonder … could I take a look?"

Her brows went a notch higher.

"I've been doing a few online queries. Just curiosity on my part." *Shut up, Charlie. Don't tell her there's a family member involved.*

She waved a hand toward the curtain. "Sure, go ahead. Don't know what there is to see."

I didn't either, but it was worth a look to orient myself to the layout of the crime scene. Accident scene. Whatever this was.

I left my purchase on the counter and stepped over to the opening in the wall. Pushing aside the plastic, I stepped through into a large space coated in plaster dust and wood chips. The room was about the same size as the tea shop. Alva had said she was doubling her space to accommodate gift items for sale. There was a cold, dark fireplace at the opposite end, and I could envision cozy fires going at each end of the finished shop, making it a warm place to come on a winter day.

To my right, windows faced the street. They'd been papered over but I imagined them revealed and cleaned, with soft curtains to match those in the rest of the shop. On my left, a pile of bricks and rubble exposed the space where the body had been discovered. Stone steps rose against the back wall of the building. I thought back to my visit to Baker Street and wished I had Sherlock's knowledge. There had to be clues scattered all over this place.

"Didn't know those were there," Alva said. She stood in the opening, holding the plastic aside with one hand. "When I leased this extra space, I only meant to replace the brick wall with plasterboard. Wanted something more modern, and the old bricks weren't in good shape, crumbling badly. Carl and Bertie said it would be easy enough to tear them down. Had no idea the brick wall had been added to close in those old stairs."

"Where do the stairs lead?" I stepped over the partly-gone brick section and craned my neck to see the top. It appeared the steps went about eight feet up and were stopped by a floor.

"There's flats above. Don't know why the stairs would've been here. They've since put the stairs on the outside—you get to the flats through the alley behind."

"I wonder how long ago that was done?" Mark Cardrick had been reported missing in 1990.

She shrugged. "Can't say. I've only had my shop here twenty years. It's been this way all along. This space I've now leased, it was a men's shoe store for a long time. Old fashioned shoemaker who'd repair a gentleman's good shoes. Before people started wearing trainers all the time. Made in China. People don't keep clothing and shoes like they used to in my grandmother's day. Wear it til it gets a little worn or dirty, replace with another cheap one."

I nodded, not admitting I'm one of those in sneakers who replaces a pair every six months or so. Her statement about being in business here *only* twenty years—it was a reminder once again about how different things are in America, where a business claims bragging rights for being around more than ten or so. And few structures outlast one or two owners—they're razed so the newest, latest entrepreneur can put in something new and start from scratch. Here, the buildings outlast generations, even centuries, of tenants.

"The old man died and his sons had no interest. They cleared out the leather shoes and classic styles, replaced 'em all with sporty styles, but I guess they couldn't compete with the prices at the bigger stores. Closed the place down at least ten years ago."

Once again, I pictured the body behind this wall. No matter how he came to land there, he'd lain in place for a very long time.

I pondered this as I walked toward the market to pick up tonight's dinner. Two blocks along, I passed La Fontana and remembered that Carlos and Maria had also been long-time friends with my aunt. Surely they'd also known Mark Cardrick. On a whim I turned and opened the front door.

Maria stood behind the bar, apparently checking the supply of ingredients for sangria. I re-introduced myself but she had already remembered me.

"Of course, Louisa's niece. Are you enjoying your visit? I'm sorry we aren't open yet." She set three large oranges on the bar beside a bottle of cognac.

"That's fine. I really just wanted to ask you some questions about your early years here in Bury. I get the impression from Louisa that you and Carlos also knew Mark Cardrick."

Her forehead wrinkled slightly.

"Louisa's boyfriend at the time ..."

"Ah, yes. My, that's been a long time ago."

"After they broke up, did you keep in touch with him?"

She shook her head. "Not at all. I don't recall actually seeing him after that. We knew Louisa was on her own again, but … How do I say this nicely? We didn't much care for Mark's company. She was the only reason we included him among our friends."

"She told me he'd lied to her and that was the reason for their split."

"I'm not surprised."

"Because …?"

She shook her head again. "Nothing specific. I'm sorry, I really shouldn't have even said this much. Their relationship was none of my business and I don't like to tell tales. I'll only say that we weren't unhappy when he moved on." She picked up a knife and began slicing the oranges.

"I got the same feeling from her." I watched in fascination as she sliced all three oranges and made short work of a lemon, all in a few seconds. She piled them into a deep bowl and doused the lot with cognac. "Did you or Carlos ever hear where he went, whether he left Bury or hung around a while longer?"

"Sorry, no. He was gone, just that quickly."

Yes, he was.

I thanked her for her time and promised to say hello to my aunt for her. For a moment when I entered the restaurant, I'd contemplated whether Maria or Carlos might have killed Cardrick, but nothing about her demeanor suggested hatred or violence toward him. They simply didn't care for his company. No crime in that.

I aimed my steps toward completion of my marketing.

Chapter 10

Voices at the front door surprised me, and I peered through from the kitchen. Louisa was talking to a young man, directing him to hang his jacket on the rack near the door.

"Charlie, I'd like you to meet one of our local authors." She placed a hand around his shoulders and almost shoved him toward me. "This is Nigel Herringbone."

I dried my hands on the towel I'd happened to be holding and reached out to shake his. I guessed him to be in his late twenties, slender, with dark hair that fell in curls over his forehead, a pale, indoor complexion, and horn-rimmed glasses. He wore tan slacks, a button-front shirt, and a navy sweater vest. Even in June.

"Nigel is a writer," Louisa bragged.

"Yes, so you said." I suppose my expression must have

registered my confusion.

"He stopped in at the office this afternoon to bring copies of his newest, *The Ghosts of Suffolk County*, and I thought it would be great fun to have dinner together."

Of course she did—this was my aunt's nature. Luckily, I had bought a roasted chicken at Marks & Spencer, and there were plenty of veggies to go with it. Fitting another person at the table wouldn't be a problem, but there went my plan for speaking to her alone.

"I did insist upon bringing along a good bottle of wine," he said, reaching for his messenger bag.

From its depths he pulled a French Bordeaux that was definitely a notch above what I normally bought. He handed me the wine and I excused myself to quickly add a third place setting at the small table and throw another handful of broccoli florets into the batch I'd just placed in the steamer. Crusty bread and a simple salad completed the meal, along with the tea cake I'd picked up from Alva's. Louisa bustled in, located three wine glasses, and uncorked the bottle.

"Dinner can be on the table in a few minutes," I told her.

"Lovely! Come, let's chat in the parlor until then. You'll find Nigel a fascinating source of information on the haunted sites of this town. Well, sites throughout the county, actually, as he's lived here his entire life and made this the subject of his dissertation."

"Wow." I actually couldn't think of a single question to ask about haunted places, but I figured Louisa could easily carry that conversational ball.

We carried our glasses into the living room, where Nigel was browsing the titles on her bookshelf.

"You have my first two books," he said with a smile.

"Oh, yes. Loved them both. And it's why I couldn't wait to get your new one." She set her glass on a small side table and picked up the book. "Would you sign it for me?"

He obligingly pulled a pen from his shirt pocket and took the book from her.

"I can't wait to read it," she said.

I meandered to the bookshelf and gazed over her collection of memorabilia. Scattered among the books, she'd placed little objects from her travels—things that leaned more toward nature than the touristy junk most people bring home. I recognized a chunk of Morenci turquoise from Arizona and the feather of a blue jay, but the other artifacts just looked like rocks. Given what she'd previously told me about visits to the tombs of Egypt and the shores of Madagascar, these could be nearly anything.

As Nigel proceeded to point out a particular chapter in his book, my gaze went to a row of photographs. Louisa with flowing blonde hair in her youth, turning white systematically as she hit her fifties and sixties. In some of the photos she was alone, posed at a famous site—the Great Pyramids in the background of one, the Leaning Tower of Pisa behind her in another. Some of the shots included fellow travelers—friends, I assumed. And in one of them I recognized the face of Mark Cardrick.

He wore jeans and a patterned yellow shirt—it could easily be the same one that clothed his skeleton, all these many years later. A chill passed over me.

Then the kitchen timer went off. I shook off the strange realization that the photo was taken near the time of his death.

"Dinner's ready," I said, motioning Louisa and Nigel toward the kitchen.

They followed and took seats at the table while I pulled the chicken from the oven and buttered the vegetables.

"This looks wonderful," Nigel said. "I'm afraid I'm rather hopeless as a cook, so it's normally Thai food takeaway for me. Having a home cooked meal is a rare treat."

"Then you shall come more often," Louisa said.

I avoided having to admit that I hadn't actually done a whole lot of cooking by changing the subject. "Did I hear Louisa say you've written three books?"

He blushed in an endearing way to prove he wasn't too full of himself. I could see why my aunt was enchanted with the young man.

"Yes, well, certainly not as an authority on the first one. I wanted to cover the history of the oldest buildings here in Bury, but of course I had no idea what a monumental undertaking that would become. I settled for what amounts to a paragraph or two on the most well-known ones." He took a bite of the chicken and nodded approval for the taste. "Researching that book was my introduction to the archives at the museum here. Do you know they've got piles of information, literally *piles* of it, for nearly all the oldest structures here?"

I could only shake my head.

"Oh yes. And the archivist—the old one who passed away a couple of years ago—" sending a glance toward Louisa, who nodded vaguely. "He was also a Nigel … Any rate, he spent his entire career searching out information, cataloguing it, and organizing it brilliantly. Anyone can go there now and request to see the records. You would be absolutely amazed at the various uses many of these buildings saw over the centuries."

Throughout this, he continued to meticulously direct food onto his fork and into his mouth, chewing and swallowing without managing to let it appear that he was talking with food in his mouth.

"As one instance, there's a bike shop on Skinner Street, which previously served as the first workshop for motorcars in the years when there were probably no more than twenty of them in the area." A chuckle at that possibility. "Before it was the auto shop it was, variously, a blacksmith's shop, a metal foundry, and a hog pen."

"The list goes on," Louisa added. "I've read your book several times."

My interest perked up. "There's a place, Brody's Tea Shop, and another retail site next to it. Do you happen to know the history of that one?"

Nigel had set down his fork to take up his wine glass. "The little place on Abbeygate Street? I believe that's the address of the first tavern in town. Actually, a tavern on the ground floor with an inn—rooms to let—on the first floor above."

"Was it? I hadn't realized," said Louisa. "Of course, the thick stone walls should have given away its age."

"Naturally, the Angel Hotel became the more famous, even in 1452 when it was built, because of the larger accommodations. The name of the old tavern is lost to history—or perhaps I've forgotten it among the tons of facts I try to keep in my head."

He reached again beneath the V neckline of his vest and dug into his shirt pocket, where he came out with a business card.

"Ask for Michael at the museum," he said, handing it to me. "With my card, he'll give you access to anything you want to know from the archives."

"Nigel's on the board of directors of the museum," Louisa said.

Despite her own adventurous life and claims to fame with her ghost tours and knowledge of the supernatural activity in the area, my aunt was clearly enthralled with tonight's last-minute guest. They continued to talk about various locales while I cleared the dishes, heated the kettle, and sliced the cake.

By bedtime, I felt as though my head were bursting with new information. I jotted a few notes I thought might pertain to my investigation. Tomorrow I would check out the museum archives.

Restless, I texted Drake to see what was going on at home. He responded with: Still up? I'll call you. My phone rang fifteen seconds later.

"We took a late lunch break," he said, "but I forgot how many hours in the time difference. Didn't want to call if you were already asleep."

"Are you still on the fire?"

"Yeah—it's a big one. Up to 30,000 acres now, so all we're doing is protecting structures wherever we can."

"I'm surprised you got a break for food."

"I'm sitting in the aircraft. Got out long enough to pee, and one of the hotshots on the crew brought me a burrito. I'll have to pull pitch in a few minutes."

I'd only worked one forest fire with him. Most of the work—dipping the water bucket, and calculating the unexpected winds that always surround a major fire—is beyond my skill level. And my protective husband doesn't want me to take the risk. The first time he said so, I felt a little resentful, but even at a distance it's scary, scary work.

I have to be grateful he wants me safe.

He asked about Louisa and I filled him in, a little.

"So tomorrow is museum day?" he asked with a chuckle. "I never quite pictured you deep in some historical archive."

"I know, right? I'll see how it goes. I could be bored to tears in minutes." I left out the fact that I really only had one mission, to find out who had occupied that building and would have had the chance to stow a body in a disused stairwell.

Chapter 11

I fell asleep in my favorite way, with loving words in my head from my husband. I woke the following morning to another rainy day, so I dressed accordingly and, after a muffin breakfast with Louisa, headed toward the museum.

The current archivist couldn't speak highly enough of the previous one, old Nigel. The neatness of the files attested to the man's dedication and—dare I call it?—obsession. No matter what prompted a guy to spend a career in the basement of the ancient stone building, sorting papers and creating files, I had to say I appreciated the efforts. My guide checked a logbook of some kind then went directly to a specific wooden file cabinet. Third drawer down, midway through the neatly organized manila folders, he came up with one labeled The MacCallum Building.

"Of course, people change the name by which they popularly call a place. But here in the archives, we always file by the oldest known name. Yours was built in the late 1500s and was called after the woman who operated the original tavern. Understand, mind you, that *tavern* sometimes stood in as a term for a brothel in those times. Or not. Actual evidence as to the purpose of the building generally doesn't go back that far."

He directed me to a table with a pair of chairs and a good reading light. "You're free to browse the folder. I can show you a bit about how we've organized the information and then leave you on your own."

"Oldest data will be at the back. That way, it's easy for us to add new material, just to drop it in the front of the file. To begin at the beginning, you'll turn the folder over and open the back cover, just so." He demonstrated. "Now, this document will be the original land plot. You'll see the streets have changed little, although at the time they were probably dirt trails which would become quite muddy. Cobblestones were added to help with that problem, normally on the most-traveled roads first. A builder would apply to the planning authority, although the required information was minimal, compared with today's complexities."

I saw a simple, handwritten page, with a short description: Stone and timber building, 20 meters by 15 meters.

"He doesn't even have to list how many windows and doorways. They often just put them in as they went, and always with an eye toward keeping out drafts and making the space habitable during the long, cold winters."

A sketch showed a simple rectangle with a fireplace

at each end, a doorway near the front corner nearest the street and another one on the back wall.

"And this is the place where Brody's Tea Shop is now located?"

"Yes'm. Right there." He traced a finger along the sketch of the street, and stabbed at the building. "The tea shop sits, I believe, at the east end of the space."

"That's what interests me most, the recent history of what businesses occupied the space for the past fifty years or so."

"Oh yes, the really new parts." He closed the folder and flipped it so the top cover was easily accessed. "Easier than moving through all these pages. Now, we can look from today backwards."

When he opened the front cover of the folder, there was a photo of Brody's. The sign was identical, although a few things looked different. Planters beside the front door were missing, and the curtains at the windows were gone.

"Old Nigel liked to tromp about town with his camera in hand, snapping everything he could think of, mostly the old buildings as they appeared in his time. Brilliant idea."

"Yes, it was. May I?"

"Absolutely. Not many—especially not many Americans—take an interest in our little world down here in the basement. Just take care not to remove anything or to shuffle the order of the documents."

I flipped the first photo over and saw a date on the back: August, 14, 2010. The next one showed the same stone façade, but the windows in this one were papered over and the door was at the opposite end of the long wall. The picture directly beneath it was the same view, although the photographer—presumably old Nigel himself—had stepped back to capture the entire building in one shot. It also showed a row of smaller windows above the two shops, the living quarters Alva had referred to. I wondered if the windows had been there from the beginning, when the place was an inn.

Following the archivist's lead, I closed the folder and turned the whole thing over before going to the back and paging forward. In front of the plot plan and builder's paperwork, there was indeed a drawing. It depicted a simple stone structure. There were chimneys at both ends, a narrow door facing the street at each end (someone must have decided two exits would be smart), and the row of narrow windows above. The windows below must have been added later. The two stories comprised the whole thing.

Again to the front, I paged past the photos I'd already seen and began digging downward. A picture dated January 12, 2000, showed the tea shop in the same place. There was a Grand Opening sign in the window. Next door was the shoe store Alva had described. Using the handy magnifying glass my archivist friend had left nearby, I could see that the shoes on display were modern sport shoes. This would have been the era when it was about to go out of business. And sure enough, the next earlier photo showed a bookshop in place of the tea shop; the shoes in the other slot were old styles. I must have misunderstood that the old shoemaker was there during the same time as the tea shop. Alva had moved in later.

I got out my notebook and jotted down the names of each of these businesses and the dates on the pictures. In a photo dated 1981, it appeared the bookstore was brand new. Before that, a 1975 photo showed a restaurant in Alva's spot, the old shoe shop next door. It wasn't until the late 1940s that I came across a picture showing one business which took up both halves of the building, a clothing store by the same name as the shoe shop.

The post-war years would have been a tough time in Britain to start a business, and that proved correct. Earlier shots showed the clothing store looking prosperous. Later, the stubborn owner must have dropped the clothing lines, walled off his retail space to half the footage, and stuck with the part he loved best—shoes. So, the dividing wall had gone up during that era.

But what about the stone staircase leading to the second story? It could have remained accessible, especially if the shoe man lived above his store, a common practice back then.

I caught the attention of my host and asked if there was a way to know the time period for interior changes.

"Nothing quite as detailed. Unfortunately, modern-day building codes are a fairly recent thing. An owner or tenant could add a wall or take one out whenever he wanted. As long as he didn't cut the electricity or water lines to a neighbor, who would care?" He gave me a puzzled look. "Might I ask, what's the reason for your curiosity?"

"There was an American, a man who may have been here in the late '80s or early 1990. He vanished and the family reported him as a missing person. I've spoken with a family member and developed a further curiosity about the case after learning about him on an internet cold case site." The explanation kept my aunt's name out of it. "He might have been here in Bury at some point."

He nodded toward the file on the MacCallum Building. "Oh, are you speaking of the skeleton that was found in

the new construction area?"
     So much for Alva's hoping this would remain low-key.

Chapter 12

I left the museum's archive room with a few pages of notes and a caution by the curator that 'old Nigel' had certainly not captured every phase in the life of every building. There was certainly a lot more to be learned in Bury St. Edmunds. He said it hopefully, probably wishing for more frequent visitors to his world of files and photographs.

Out on the street, the rain had stopped and a bright summer day was unfolding as the clouds scudded away. I found myself heading toward the gardens, my newfound favorite place to chow down on one of those yummy Cornish pasties and think. But before I'd reached the pasty shop, my feet turned toward Brody's. I *could* enjoy a lunch there and perhaps quiz her some more. On the other hand, I'd already been there twice—perhaps more could be learned from other sources. I consulted my list.

Alva Brody was still my most convenient source so I headed in her direction. The tea shop was busier than I'd seen it, obviously at the height of the lunch hour. Most of the customers appeared to be shop girls and mothers with young children, here to eat quickly and be on their way to work or home, although I spotted the two workmen, Carl and Bertie, at a table. It made sense that Alva might prefer them not to be hammering and creating extra dust during her busiest hour of the day.

It wasn't long before I got a table after placing my order for a salad. Alva had an extra waitress today, but she was still working full speed, delivering plates to tables, working the till, and filling bakery orders.

I lingered over my salad and consulted my notes from my morning's research. Although the museum archive held an amazing amount of information, there were still large gaps in time. If I could get a lead or two, I hoped one thread would lead to another. Like unraveling an old sweater, the resulting clues might wind up being sizeable. And then I would approach Louisa and ask again. It seemed impossible that, so far, she and her circle from Spain had been the only people in Bury who had known the victim.

Near the door, I sensed a change in the energy in the room. DS Redding and DC Edwards had come back. They gave me a brief nod, spoke in low tones to Alva, who tipped her head in the direction of Carl and Bertie's table. With no more than a nod toward the workmen, the two cops walked toward the plastic curtain and pushed it aside to enter the construction area.

Alva stopped at my table to ask if I'd like a refill on my water. "Heard it this morning," she said quietly. "They've caught the killer."

What! My mind leaped to the other side of that curtain.

"In that society case. It was the doctor himself, killed his wife for her inheritance money." She poured water into my glass, her eyes drifting to where the police had gone.

"That didn't take long," I said.

She scoffed. "Them fancy pants, educated types. Just 'cause a man's got a medical degree, doesn't mean he's got a lick of smarts about covering his tracks. What I heard, they knew it was him right from the start. Injected her with enough sedative to put down a horse, is what they're saying."

I'd only caught a couple of the news headlines and that had been the speculation. Crimes of passion aren't usually well planned. And it seemed the local police certainly weren't wasting any time at getting back around to the skeleton in the wall. It might not take them long to learn the victim's identity and connect him with my aunt.

Or with me, for that matter. I wondered if my little visits to the coroner's office and the history archives would come to light. If I wanted to keep ahead of them, I'd better get busy.

From my seat, I could see only vague shapes moving around in the room behind the curtain. After a few minutes one of the cops stepped into the tearoom and motioned to Carl and Bertie. The two workers followed him, and it appeared each cop took one of them aside so they couldn't compare answers.

Other than myself and one pair of elderly ladies, the rest of the customers had left. I gathered my things and caught up with Alva at the till in front.

"I was hoping to talk with you, to get a little more information about the history of the building's tenants."

Her nervous glance toward the other room told me that wasn't going to happen now.

I was really beginning to feel stuck. "Maybe later? Could I—?"

Male voices interrupted. The two detectives walked up to the counter. I received my change and walked out when Redding gave me a stern look. But I was dying of curiosity. What were they asking Alva? How far along were they with the case?

I gave one last glance toward the tea shop before continuing to the Abbey Gardens where I would review my notes. I also knew it was time to talk to Louisa again, and I couldn't let her off the hook with cute stories about her adventurous past. She tended to drift through life savoring the current adventure. That might not be a bad thing, but there were times a person had to keep self-preservation in mind.

The teashop closed at five, I remembered from the sign on the front door. I spent the few intervening hours walking through the streets and memorizing the shops I passed. All of them had an air of permanence but I realized how deceptive that could be. Clearly, from the historical records, businesses came and went in this town just as in any other. Only as a tourist did I see them in snapshot mode, feeling they had always existed in place and always would.

When Alva stepped out her front door at 5:05 and turned to lock the door I followed for half a block then pounced. She didn't seem especially surprised to see me.

"So what's your interest in all this, then?" she asked as we walked side by side toward the Corn Exchange building.

"I've learned who the victim was, and I have reason to

think a relative of mine knew him. I'm completely certain she had nothing to do with his death, but she could be the person the police focus on. Please, it's important that I find out as much as possible so I can send them toward the real killer if they come after her."

I hoped she didn't think I was some looney. I probably sounded that way.

"And what are you wanting that you think I can tell you?"

"Just your memories of the place and the time. Can you tell me about some of the other businesses that occupied the building—both your space and the one you're moving into?"

"I'll remember better on a pint of ale," she said, a little smile softening her features.

She pointed to the Duck and Dog sign just ahead and we went inside. While I ordered at the bar she found a table in a back corner, away from the growing crowd that was cheering two men in an intense dart game.

I set our glasses on the table, along with a bowl of peanuts. We gave a little 'cheers' with the raised glasses, and I let a moment go by. "You've lived here in Bury all your life? It must be something, being in the midst of all this history."

"I suppose I don't know any other way. It's just how the town is."

"Still, I found pictures in the archives showing lots of changes over time. The various uses one building can see in the span of years."

She nodded. "True enough. So, you wanted to know about the MacCallum Building and I don't know that I can tell you much."

"Just let your mind wander back over the years and tell me what you do remember."

"Well, when I was a girl I recall there being a card and stationery store. Mum would take me each year to choose a birthday card for my best friend, Iris."

"Do you remember who owned the card store?"

"She was an old lady. But her hair was dark, so she might have been forty." Alva chuckled. "Funny how age is such a relative thing."

I had to agree. I'd once thought turning thirty was a momentous event.

"Do you remember her name, and do you think she's still around?"

"Oh, heavens. That was fifty years ago. I don't even recall what happened to the shop."

It was before the time I was most concerned with anyway. "Moving a little more recently—what occupied the space after the card shop?"

"Oh, the place was filled with furniture and lighting fixtures and such for awhile. That one occupied the whole building. I was entranced by the pieces—we called them 'mod' at the time. Thinking back, there were sofas in horrendous shades of lime green and orange. But I was quite young then, too, certainly not in the market to buy my own furniture."

I jotted a few details to refresh my memory later, when all this would begin to blur.

"And for a little while, I think a pet groomer opened up. But it's really much more space than one needs for clipping and brushing little doggies, don't you think? I suppose the rent proved too high, as well. I never knew the owner of that one. But I do remember it being a boutique clothing store when I was a young woman. I absolutely loved going in there and browsing. I bought a red sweater there once. My mother thought it was scandalous, me wearing red! But I loved it and would wear it out on dates when she didn't know."

"That was in the space where your teashop is now?"

"No, no. That would have been next door. The bookstore was in the spot where I am now. That was in the days before any such thing as a chain bookstore."

"And the owners of those shops? Are they still around?" I really felt we were getting warmer—the timeframe was much closer.

"Oh yes. Clive Marlowe owned the bookstore, and the Marlowes are definitely still around. The son went into real estate and owns the biggest agency in town. The bookstore seemed in a bit of a financial bind at one time, as I recall …" Her gaze went toward the ceiling for a moment. "Or maybe I'm thinking of the other shop. It must have been, because Marlowe's Bookshop is still here. They have a good location on Angel Lane. Of course, Waterstone's came in and has the larger store."

"And the boutique? Is it long gone?"

"The owner is still here and has another store. It's still the trendy clothing the younger people like. She moved, ages ago, to a prime spot on Butter Market. Angelica Smith is her name. I always loved that, compared to my own very plain name. *Angelica* sounded foreign and exotic. I'm sure she's middle-aged by now, but she's kept up with fashion. Loves it."

Alva drained the last of her ale. I was furiously scribbling notes.

"Well, I must be off. Reggie will be wanting his dinner."

She stood and I thanked her profusely.

I looked back over what I'd written, filling in gaps while the information was fresh in my head. I had a boutique, a bookstore, a card shop, a pet groomer, and a home furnishings store, in addition to the shoe store and bicycle shop that were much further in the past. It seemed a good start. Hopefully, one of them could tell me something about the hidden stairwell.

Chapter 13

I didn't want to ambush Louisa so I waited until we'd finished dinner and were having a glass of wine in the parlor before I brought up the subject.

"The local police are investigating that skeleton. They came in while I was having lunch at Brody's today."

She ran a hand through her curls, her eyes bright and attentive, but she made no comment and her body seemed relaxed.

"They're going to find out if it's Mark Cardrick."

"I wonder … perhaps it is."

"You aren't the least bit concerned? We've already discovered you were probably one of the last people to see him."

"Yes. Alive." She slugged back a bit more of the wine than she was used to, choking a little.

"The last time we talked about him, you told me you lived together for a while and parted on somewhat of a bad note."

"I did? I don't recall our last words."

That didn't exactly jibe with what I remembered but I let it drop.

"Where did you live? Was it here, in this house?"

"No, being that I had barely landed in Bury myself, I was renting a flat."

I waited, staring expectantly.

"Oh, you mean where was the flat? Um, it was above a small clothing store. You accessed the apartments above by some back stairs from the alley."

"Did this happen to be on the same street where Brody's Tea Shop is now?" I felt as if I were having to pry every bit of information out of her. It was so unlike my aunt not to launch into a story at the drop of a hat.

She glanced upward, thinking. "Yes, actually. And there was another shop next to it."

"Alva Brody told me about those stores, said both have moved to other parts of town."

"I seem to remember the bookshop was struggling. I suppose times improved."

"What else do you remember about it, about the place you lived or the circumstances when Mark left?"

"Oh, not much. I didn't stay in that flat long. It was about the time I got the job caring for old Mrs. Whitmere, and that's when I moved into this house."

I remembered she'd told me the elderly woman had no other heirs and had left Louisa the house when she died. That was the explanation as to why all the furnishings and fittings were so 1950s—the old woman hadn't changed a thing in her years here, and apparently Louisa was content with them as well.

I set my wine glass down and took her hands. "Louisa, this is important. When Mark Cardrick was reported missing, the police talked to you. What types of questions were they asking?"

"Police? I don't recall being interrogated. Surely, I would remember *that*. There may have been someone who came around, asking about the flat. Maybe that's when his name came up. It certainly wasn't a formal inquiry, not at all. I would have opened the place up and told them to look all they wanted." She patted my arm and reached again for her glass. Discovering it empty, she stood and headed for the kitchen.

Was my aunt starting to experience some memory issues? She was not yet seventy, but I suppose those things can happen. But then I remembered the vivid details she'd given of other events close to that time, her travels through Spain and Morocco. No, she simply didn't want to talk about this whole issue of Mark Cardrick and their past.

I only hoped she would open up to me before the police came to question her. If I had better leads, I could find a motive for another suspect. As it was, all I knew was that Louisa and Mark had lived together and they'd parted on bad terms.

Those facts would surely make her a prime suspect.

I spent a restless night, wrestling with my conscience over a thought that had come to me after the evening's conversation. She said she would have let the police search her apartment. What if they'd been inclined to do so— what would they have found?

Shortly after dawn I heard Louisa arise. Sounds came

through—the bath and footsteps going down the stairs—while I lay quietly in my bed, waiting.

When the small kitchen noises abated and I heard the front door open, I got up and stepped over to my bedroom window that faced the street. Below, she walked away toward her office, a happy spring to her step, her shoulder bag bouncing against her hip.

So innocent. She *must* be.

I quickly dressed in jeans and a T-shirt, went into the kitchen and fortified myself with a large mug of coffee, allowing a fifteen-minute window for her to arrive and settle at her office, in case she'd forgotten something and returned home, before I began my treachery.

Although it felt wrong, searching her house, I had to know. And she had always told me to look for anything I needed, to help myself. If there were letters or other memorabilia from the time of her relationship with Mark, I might learn whether my aunt could possibly be tied to his death. Once they focused on her, the police would come and seize everything and my chance would be lost.

At least that's what I told myself—had told myself all night long.

I started with the parlor. Below the shelf with the framed photos I'd noticed earlier, there were a couple of photo albums. I pulled them off the shelf and went to the sofa. Turning on a lamp, I studied Louisa's image in the picture on the shelf, the one she had identified as herself and Cardrick in London. Her blonde curls fell in soft waves to her shoulders, a very similar style to what she still wore, although the strands were mostly white now.

I opened the first album, looking for photos that would establish the time frame. These began with Louisa at a much younger age. In her twenties, most likely. She'd once told me about going along on a dig to the tombs of Egypt at the age of twenty-seven. And there she was, posed among a team of young people with shovels and sieves.

This was silly. Naturally, photo albums would only show what she didn't mind sharing with the world. I turned the album upside down, hoping a letter or two might fall out. Nothing. And the other album netted the same.

A cupboard below the shelves was filled with tablecloths and napkins, a pair of silver candlesticks, two boxes of napkin rings—still sealed in the packaging, obviously an unused gift from someone. There were serving bowls, a gravy boat, and a huge soup tureen in a pattern of tiny roses that I couldn't imagine Louisa purchasing, not in my wildest dreams. All of this had to be part of the previous owner's legacy.

A quick glance behind each closed cabinet door in the parlor, kitchen, and downstairs hall showed more of the same. Just the ordinary stuff everyone has, and most of it from a bygone era. Not one mysterious cardboard box, not one locked safe, not even a shoebox labelled Love Letters. She might not have saved much from her own past, but neither had she taken the time to go through the older woman's possessions and declutter.

Still, I should look upstairs.

Skipping the guest room, which I could search to my heart's content any time, I went into Louisa's room. I got a big twinge of guilt, but I needed to work quickly. She would only be at the office a half day, and it wouldn't do to be caught with my hands in places they shouldn't be.

Where did women stash their treasured memories? An

old fashioned ladies dressing table caught my eye. It had two banks of small drawers, divided by a low shelf with a knee space for the woman who would sit on the spindle-legged little bench at the center, using the triple mirror at eye level to apply her makeup and style her hair. I almost laughed at the image of Louisa doing much of anything in the hair and makeup department, but she might use those six little drawers as the perfect place to keep old cards and letters.

Unfortunately not. There was an array of combs and barrettes, some night cream in a jar that actually was new, two nail files, and three drawers entirely devoted to scarves. I pawed through them, resisting the urge to pull them out and imagine my aunt dressing up and matching the scarves with her outfits. The main thing was, there were no letters.

Same with the armoire, which held a dozen skirts and the floaty tops she preferred. The top shelf had sandals in shoeboxes—only two pair—and the floor of the cabinet contained two pair of boots. I could take some lessons on decluttering my own closets based on this.

Surely, she didn't keep old love letters in the bathroom. I skipped that.

A trap door in the ceiling in the upstairs hall caught my attention. Of course, an old house like this would have an attic. Not convinced I wanted to go there, I nevertheless found a chair and stepped up to get my fingers into the recessed place that acted as a means of grabbing the door.

It took quite a tug but eventually the hinges began to screech and the door slowly gave way. Then it happened all at once.

The door banged me on the head, built-in stairs came sliding down, a rain of dust and cobwebs filled my hair, and something fell out and smacked my shoulder. A dead bat.

Chapter 14

I think I screamed something like "I am out of here!" except that it included a good long string of curse words. I shoved the whole ladder/trapdoor assembly back in place, then went to find the sweeper to clean up the dusty mess on the hall carpet.

Done. I am so done with searching.

It took a half hour, but I finally cleared the evidence of my foolish foray into places that were none of my business. I took a long shower and double-shampooed my hair, which still felt as if it had cobweb strands in it.

It's what you deserved, dweeb. Going through someone's personal stuff is not cool.

Okay, conscience, you're right. But she said …

Not that I'd never invaded someone's privacy before—just not someone I knew and loved. And what had I hoped to accomplish, anyway? If I'd found angry letters between Louisa and Mark, was I going to hide them from the police? Confront her? Burn them? I actually couldn't see any of those things happening, so it was just as well that I'd struck out.

I wasn't sure whether that was a comforting thought, or not, as I changed into clean clothing and headed out the door. There was time for a little more investigating—on someone else's turf—and then I would stop by the tourism office and take Louisa to lunch when her work day ended. I might not ever tell her why, but my conscience might be a tiny bit assuaged.

As I walked toward the shopping district, I mentally reviewed what I'd learned yesterday from the archive guy and from Alva Brody. So, when I found myself staring at the sign for Marlowe's Books, it seemed as good a place to start as any.

It was the same store I'd wandered into my first day in town, the place I bought the Rankin book I'd barely started reading. How had I not noticed the charming façade on the shop, the carved lintel and door frame, and the old-fashioned window display? Outside, the light posts flanking the property resembled gas lamps, and each sported a planter basket overflowing with petunias. There was an English-ness to it that made me think of something straight out of Dickens. I stepped up from sidewalk level and opened the heavy mahogany door.

The same old man sat behind the counter; he barely looked up when I walked in. As there seemed to be no point in pretending to browse and then hitting him with a casual question, I went right to him.

"Are you Mr. Marlowe?"

He nodded, looking as if he expected to deal with

someone who wanted to return the book they'd rushed through reading the night before.

"I was speaking with Alva Brody at the tea shop yesterday and she said your bookstore used to be in that location."

"That's right."

"I wonder if you might remember this man, from back in that time," I said, locating the photo of Mark Cardrick from the Sleuths website I had saved to my phone.

"Hmph, that was a long time ago." He barely glanced at the picture.

I stretched the photo to make the face larger. "Could you just take a look? He was reported as a missing person and the family is still worried."

Not exactly the truth, that second part, but I had a feeling it wouldn't do to bring up the fact that Cardrick was dead.

"And what's this got to do with me?" he asked, looking at the photo and shaking his head.

"I don't know. That's why I'm asking. Just wondered if you might have had contact with him back in the early '90s."

"Never saw him," he said, handing back my phone.

Something in his face had closed down. Maybe he was lying; maybe he was just irritated at the uppity American barging into his shop and asking questions. I couldn't be sure.

From a back room I heard some shuffling and a groan. A gray-haired woman, carrying a heavy-looking box, waddled in.

"Clive, honestly sweetheart, I could use a hand back there. The shipment's come in."

He stepped toward his wife and took the box, which he deposited on the back counter. "You shouldn't be lifting those, what with your back and all."

"Where's our Scotty? He knows—" She noticed me for the first time. "Oh, sorry. Didn't realize we've a customer."

Clive had dutifully headed toward the back room.

I waved off the apology, introducing myself. "No problem. I was just …" A thought occurred to me. "I was just asking Mr. Marlowe about this man who may have been around back in the days when your shop was over on Abbeygate Street."

I tapped my phone to life and showed her the photo, which she studied intently for a minute.

"Oh, yes, him. My lord, that must have been thirty years ago. Look at the hairstyle and that shirt."

I chuckled. "True." I would have been in elementary school and could only imagine some of the outfits I'd worn then.

"He was a looker, that one." She blushed a little. "We were all of us a lot younger then."

Clive came back with an even larger box than the one Sarah had carried in. He sent her a firm look and she quickly handed my phone back.

I wandered away and pretended to browse the shelves, letting them carry on as if I wasn't there, but their conversation stuck strictly to the business at hand. No mentions of the photo or the past.

I selected a local history book, full of pictures of Bury St. Edmunds. If Louisa didn't already have it, this would make a nice hostess gift. If, as I suspected, she already owned every book pertaining to the town, I would take it home and show Drake what he'd missed out on.

Leaving the shop a few minutes later, I pondered the reactions of the couple. He claimed to have never seen Cardrick; she blushed. Interesting. Maybe Cardrick had been a womanizer all around town.

I couldn't quite put it together though. In the same way you can never imagine your parents having sex, it was hard to envision the elderly, stocky Sarah Marlowe in an affair. Much less with the dashing world traveler, Mark Cardrick. I needed to realize thirty years had passed and get over my stereotypes about older people and their romantic intentions.

That resolution got tested as soon as I stopped in at Angelica's Boutique, two streets over from the bookshop.

Angelica had to be in her mid-fifties but she dressed and moved with the assurance of a thirty-year-old. She was at the top of a ladder when I walked in, and it looked as though she'd carried a mannequin up, herself, and posed it on a display shelf that ran around the perimeter of the shop, a good ten feet above the sales floor.

"What do you think of the jeggings with the red sweater?" she asked.

Seeing as how the mannequin wore a blue minidress, I could only guess the woman was referring to her own attire.

"I like it."

"Have a look around—let me know if you want to try on something."

While the woman descended the ladder, I browsed a rack of cute tops in styles I suspected hadn't quite reached the American Southwest yet.

"Are you Angelica Smith?" I asked.

"Well, my close friends call me Gellie, my customers

call me Angelica, and the tax man calls me by my full name."

I laughed. "Well, I'm certainly not the tax man."

She dusted her hands on her fitted leggings and extended one toward me. "I guessed. American, aren't you?"

"Yes, and I'm conducting an investigation into a missing person." I'd decided this line worked best, since I had no authority to look into a murder.

I pulled out my phone once more and showed her the photo.

"Mark Cardrick … wow. That's a blast from the past, as they say."

"You knew him?"

"Oh, yes." She stared at the photo a moment longer. "Oh, my, I was so young. A silly girl, really."

"Was there a romance …?" I tried to add a little wink-nudge to the question.

"At the time I sort of wished there was. He was quite a lot older—nearly forty, I suppose—and my father would have had a fit. Seeing as it was my father financing my first shop at the time, I had to be smart about it." She handed the phone back and waved a hand. "Oh, who am I kidding? I was as gullible as any twenty-year-old, and he was charming, personable, outgoing. He made friends everywhere he went. We had some laughs, Mark and I."

"Do you remember the last time you saw him? Where and when?"

Angelica had walked to her sales desk, where she picked up a pricing gun and studied the roll of stickers she was loading into it.

"Let me think. Here in Bury, of course. He flitted about

the country some—up to Cambridge, out to the seaside at Ipswich now and then—but I never did. Had my hands full with my shop, and my parents were still keeping a close eye, you know."

"But he lived here—this was his base?"

"Yes ..." She stared upward for a few seconds, remembering. "Although I never actually saw his place. We always met up at the pub or somewhere."

Interesting, considering he'd lived with Louisa right above Angelica's shop for awhile. I supposed he could have had an eye out for the younger woman and arranged 'coincidental' meetings when convenient.

She proceeded to slap price stickers on the tags attached to a pile of T-shirts on the counter.

"What was his reason for moving here?" I asked. "He was American. Did he have a work visa or something?"

Her brow furrowed. "I don't think so. What was the story, then ...? He'd come here looking for someone ... He seemed to have business at the bank sometimes." Her breath chuffed out in frustration. "I just don't remember now. It was nothing to do with me. As I said, we'd meet up at the pub, catch a movie now and then. He made friends easily, so there were always a group of us."

"Can you think of anyone else I might speak to, people in the group?"

"Clarice. Have you located her yet?"

I shook my head.

"Clarice Hutchings. My bestie back then and we still see each other sometimes, although life just gets busier and more complicated as the years go by. Oh, Clarice had it bad for Mark."

"Clarice—how can I reach her?"

"Most likely at home." She scribbled a number on a sticky note and handed it to me. "She married a few years after Mark was no longer around and now she's completely into being a grandmother. That daughter of hers has her minding the baby ever since she got that *corporate* job. It involves travel."

I thanked her and ended up buying a really cute T-shirt. This investigation was starting to add to my credit card load. Walking back toward the tourism office, I pondered all the new information. Someone had told me something crucial. I just couldn't yet put my finger on what it was.

Chapter 15

Logic told me that if Mark Cardrick came to Bury St. Edmunds looking for someone, it was likely Louisa. They'd met in Spain and had a little history together. As far as I knew, he had no such history with anyone else here.

As far as I knew.

That was the big question—what *didn't* I know? A lot, I suspected.

I could make some educated guesses, though. I'd just witnessed Angelica's obvious infatuation with the man, and even blushing Sarah Marlowe who was twenty years older than the young Angelica had been back then.

Perhaps that was the simple explanation for Louisa's and Mark's breakup—too many women. Mark might have been a womanizer, or merely a flirt, and maybe Louisa had simply had her fill. She'd told me they 'had words.'

I stepped off a curb, forgetting to look to my right, and jumped backward when a tiny car beeped at me. I'll never get used to traffic coming from the wrong direction.

Back to Louisa and Mark—I pondered some more as I passed the Angel Hotel. I could see him (possibly) as a cheater, but I definitely didn't see Louisa as the clingy type. She would have just turned him loose. And that's most likely exactly what she'd done. Plus, my proving she was jealous would only hurt her case if the police should end up on this line of questioning.

So, what other direction could I look?

Unless … what if Louisa wasn't the jealous one but someone else was? Any of the other women with an eye on Mark might have wanted more of a commitment from him. Maybe whoever it was pressed him, and there was an argument that ended with a push down the stairs. I would definitely keep a closer eye on the women I interviewed and pay attention.

At the moment, though, here was the tourism office and I would chat with my aunt over lunch and see where that led us.

Where it led surprised me completely. I walked into the tourism office and she greeted me enthusiastically, her bag already over her shoulder.

"Guess who one of our newest members is?" she asked. Without waiting for an answer from my completely puzzled brain, she said, "Green Leaf Day Spa."

I was still drawing a blank.

"The owner came in to leave brochures that we can pass out to visitors, *and* … she wanted someone from the office to come and try the facilities. The better to talk it up to the guests, I suppose. So, you and I have an afternoon pass. Massages, facials, the whole works. We'll even have our lunch there. They have a complete smoothie and juice bar, according to the brochure. It sounds divine, doesn't it?"

Before I could say "I guess so," we were on our way. A quick stop by the house to grab swimsuits and we arrived at Green Leaf a half hour later. The young woman at the desk had clearly been briefed to give us the VIP tour.

The women's locker room was state of the art, with shampoos and body washes from a designer label. Once we changed into our suits, they recommended that we visit the steam room to detoxify the skin, followed by a cold plunge beneath the ten-foot waterfall. Back to hot water in the bubbling spa, then into robes and out to the loungers in the central room, with ample time to lie back and enjoy the piped-in soft piano music.

Our personal attendants would be standing by to escort us to each of the amenities, and would be happy to bring us something from the juice bar while we relaxed.

I was beginning to get more into the spirit of this thing as we walked through the beautifully appointed rooms, each decorated with classy tile work and stylish chrome fixtures. Live plants added to the ambiance in the waterfall room, and hidden diffusers distributed the scents of essential oils.

Back at the dressing room, we left our things in numbered lockers and put on our suits. Louisa enjoyed the steam room so much it was a good thing the attendant showed up to take us on to the next place. I was more than ready for the cold plunge after beginning to feel about as red as a steamed lobster. Once the cold waterfall took my breath away, I was easily led back to the warmth of the round spa tub.

"So, how did you spend your morning, dear?" Louisa asked, over the sound of the vigorous bubbles.

"I met Clive and Sarah Marlowe who own the bookstore."

"Did you? At their shop?"

"Yes, it looks like the two of them are still doing a lively business there."

"I'm surprised. They were talking of retiring ages ago, hoping their son would take over the shop."

"I think I saw him there once, but he didn't seem to actually work there."

She nodded thoughtfully. "Actually, that part doesn't surprise me. Scott Marlowe never really took an interest in the family business. He sees himself as a big, fancy real estate tycoon or some such."

The timer on our bubbling cauldron turned off and our attendants were standing there with robes for each of us. Wrapped in snuggly terrycloth, we followed our escorts to two lounge chairs. Surrounded by a jungle of plants and with a blue pool and waterfall to stare at, it felt as though we'd landed in a tropical paradise.

The smoothies we'd ordered earlier from the menu magically appeared on the small round table between us.

"Seems the middle of the day in the middle of the week is the ideal time to be here," Louisa commented, sipping from her deep green mint-chamomile drink.

She was right—we had the place to ourselves. I stirred the foam on top of my blueberry mix called Blue Lavender Bliss and tasted it. Pure fruity heaven.

"I met Angelica at the boutique," I told her. "She seems like a bundle of energy, even in later middle age."

Louisa gave me a sideways look and cleared her throat.

"I beg your pardon," she said with a mischievous grin. "I am hardly out of middle age myself. Angelica is practically a child still."

I laughed. By that reasoning, I supposed I was still in kindergarten. "Sorry. You know what I mean. And you're a bundle of energy, too. I never said otherwise."

"Touché." She held out her glass and we clicked them. "I will be even more so when I finish this smoothie. I ordered the one packed with every good-for-you nutrient on the planet."

"Were all of you friends back then?" I asked, switching back to our earlier topic. "Angelica, you and Mark? The Marlowe's?"

She adjusted the turban that was futilely trying to keep her wavy hair under control. "Of course. Everyone in Bury is friendly—at least on the surface."

As if this were a given. Maybe in this town, in that era, it was.

"But not socially, really. Mark and I were sort of free spirits. I found waitressing work wherever I went. It's a valuable skill, I'll tell you. No matter where you go, food needs to be served and it's hard for restaurants to keep good help. The hours were flexible a lot of the time, so Mark and I could head off for little side trips and adventures. The others, of course, were tied to their shops. I don't recall that we socialized much."

Angelica's words came back to me: *We'd meet up at the pub, catch a movie now and then.* Perfect spur of the moment activities for a man whose woman worked the dinner shift.

"Louisa ... I don't know quite how to ask this ..."

She gave me a frank stare. "Just spit it out."

"Did you have reason to think Mark may have cheated on you?"

"Cheated? Seems like such a middle-class term. We weren't married or anything even close."

"Well, you know … Since you lived together, I assumed there must have been some …"

"Like, were we *going steady* or something? Now that really would be a term from the past."

Sheesh. How was I messing this up so badly? "You know what I mean."

She reached out and patted my hand. "You're right, sweetheart. I didn't mean to tease. And I know I was living a sort of risky lifestyle then. By the '90s AIDS was a thing. Treatments were barely on the horizon, and it certainly wasn't considered the chronic illness it is today. We all had to be careful about sleeping around."

"Which brings me back to … do you think Mark slept around?" I wiped a sheen of moisture from my glass. "I'll just ask it straight out. You said that you and he 'had words' before he left. Is that what the argument was about?"

Her head leaned back into the lounger and she expelled a long breath. "Oh, heavens no. It was about money."

Okay. That made sense. The top three topics of fights among couples are fidelity, money, and children. My free-spirited aunt and her adventurer boyfriend weren't such a unique pair after all.

Chapter 16

Throughout the evening I thought about our conversation at the spa, although I had to admit the massage and facial did a lot to put those thoughts into the category of 'mild interest' rather than 'items of concern.' By morning, I had to pause to remember where I'd been in my investigation.

I put on jeans and the new T-shirt I'd bought at Angelica's Boutique. The note with Clarice Hutchings' phone number fell out of the bag.

Even though Louisa wasn't the jealous type, it didn't mean Clarice wasn't. Angelica told me Clarice 'had it bad' for Mark, and that could mean nearly anything. I dialed the number. When it went to voicemail, I left a brief message to the effect that Angelica Smith had suggested I call. I swear I put my sweetest, least threatening tone in it, but two hours later I still hadn't received a call back. I tried again.

And so it went through the morning. Maybe she recognized my number as foreign and felt suspicious. Finally, I picked up Louisa's landline in the house and dialed from there. Clarice picked up on the third ring, and I could hear children's voices in the background.

"Oh, yes, sorry I didn't get back," she said when I told her who I was. "It's been rather chaotic here this morning, and I've promised the children we could go to McDonald's for lunch so …"

Meeting in a public place would be better anyway. Hopefully it would put her at ease that I wasn't someone trying to con my way into her home.

"I only have a few questions, and Angelica really thought you might be of help with our inquiry. Would it be all right if I met you at McDonald's? We could get this out of the way in a few minutes, and I'm always up for a Big Mac."

The levity had the desired effect. She chuckled and said she would be there in about fifteen minutes. I would know her as the rather harried woman with three little ones, the youngest still in nappies.

I gave it twenty minutes. At home I've watched Sally with her kids. Nothing ever goes as smoothly as you think it will. I was outside, trying to peer discreetly through the front windows, when a blonde woman pulled up in a small car. From the back seat emerged two toddlers who were probably twins, about four years old—other than being of different genders, they looked nearly identical in size and coloring. Clarice ordered them to stand with one hand touching the car while she unstrapped the baby from a complicated seat in the back.

"Now," she announced to the older ones, "we shall proceed indoors in an orderly manner."

Either this woman was a drill sergeant in private, or English kids were the best-behaved I'd ever seen. They actually followed instructions, while she balanced the baby on one hip and slung a big tote bag over the other shoulder.

I stepped forward and held the door, introducing myself as she passed.

"Nice job of keeping them organized," I commented. "My receptionist could take some lessons."

"Oh, it's a simple matter," Clarice said. "If they follow every instruction, they get an ice cream after. If not, they don't. I'm quite good at keeping track and it only takes withholding the treats once or twice."

Sally really could take lessons.

"We can take that table in the front corner," Clarice suggested. "Would you mind grabbing that highchair just there?"

I can take orders just like any good kid, so I did. We got everyone set up at the table and I offered to go to the counter to place orders for all.

"It's complicated. Let me just order yours, if you don't mind sitting with the kids?"

I put on a smile and said, "Certainly." The lengths I'll go to just for an interview. I sat with the baby on my left, the little girl on my right, and the boy across the table.

"Why do you have such a funny accent?" he immediately asked.

"Well, I suppose that's because I'm from America."

Both of the twins giggled. "We saw *Frozen*. We know what Americans sound like."

I raised my eyebrows.

"But it sounds funny coming from a real person."

"In America we really like British accents, like yours."

Massive giggles again. "We don't speak with an accent. You do."

Luckily, Clarice returned, laden with a tray, before the rest of us had to pursue the argument about accents. She handed out Happy Meals and cautioned there would be no talking while eating. My Big Mac looked exactly like the ones at home, and although the fries were called chips, they looked and tasted the same too.

Clarice had bought the smallest hamburger for herself, and she pulled bites off the bun to put on the highchair tray.

"I fed her before we left the house. So much easier than trying to juggle along jars of her food and manage a two-handed burger for myself."

"Wow. This takes a lot of planning."

She shrugged as she munched a large bite of her own burger. The twins each ate roughly half of their chicken nuggets, one or two of the apple slices, and two sips of milk before they began to be antsy in their seats.

"Go play on the maze," Clarice told them. "Ten minutes!"

She turned to me. "Luckily, I have the twins only once a week. My son's wife is taking some online courses, but there's classroom time on Thursdays. My daughter, well, her job is quite demanding, so little Fiona is with me every day."

"Angelica mentioned that." I set down the remains of my Big Mac and reached for the fries. "I'll keep this quick, since you're on a ten-minute limit. I'm investigating a missing person's case, an American named Mark Cardrick.

It seems he was living here in Bury the last anyone knew."

"Mark Cardrick … That's a name from the distant past."

I smiled encouragement. "Yes. I've run into several people who remember him. Angelica said he was quite attractive. Sounded like several of the girls might have been interested in him?"

Her eyes went a little dreamy. "He was. Wavy black hair and such vivid blue eyes. And, of course, that catchy American accent. He said he was a drummer with a band back in the States and they'd recorded several albums."

I didn't remember Louisa mentioning that part. Then again, maybe Mark presented a slightly different version of himself to each woman, as needed.

"But it was the smile that captured my heart. You know, the dimple on one side, one cuspid just a little crooked. And bright white teeth." She sipped from her straw. "Does that sound stupid? My remembering silly details like that? Don't get me wrong—I've been a happily married woman for nearly thirty years now. My Archie, he's the best and I love him a hundred percent."

I nodded. I didn't see any harm in her remembering a cute guy from the past, even though she was completely in love with her husband.

"You must have married shortly after that time—back when you knew Mark?"

"Probably. Archie and I, we've known each other since primary school. Our settling down together was always a given."

"But Mark …"

"Couldn't even call it a fling. A big infatuation, sure, yeah. But there was something else I spotted in him. Something sort of … well, underhanded. It sounds disloyal to say it. But what loyalty do I have to Mark Cardrick, really?" She put a french fry on the tray for the baby, who snatched it up in her fist and proceeded to gnaw on one end. "Hard to say exactly, but there seemed to be some sort of dishonesty about him. I never quite believed the drummer story. A few other things. He'd go out with Angelica and me and some others, but I think he was living with someone else at the time. What kind of way is that to treat her? Or us?"

"Was anyone angry enough with him to really get into a huge fight over it? Jealousy can run very strong."

"Amongst my friends, I don't think so. None of us took him all that seriously. He was a fun time, but that was it."

Hadn't Louisa said something similar about Mark? A fun time but not a guy to get very serious about.

The twins emerged from the play area and pounced back into their chairs. Having an appetite now, they worked earnestly on the rest of their food, but Clarice sent me a cautionary shake of her head. "Little ears," she mouthed. True—my limited amount of time around kids had shown me they'll repeat anything they hear, usually at exactly the wrong time and place.

I had pretty much covered my questions for now, so I finished my burger and dug into my purse for money to reimburse Clarice for my meal. Thanking her, I left before I could get roped into ice cream time or holding someone's sticky little hand while the others used the bathroom.

The afternoon was beautiful, with a high-overcast sky and warm air. The walk back to Louisa's would do me good, and I found a circuitous route different from the way I'd come before. I found myself slightly turned around, as I got into some winding lanes of residential streets.

I was about to backtrack, to find the straight grid-like streets in the business district, so I could spot a route I recognized, when I came upon a familiar name. A large house with pale tan plaster and upper timbers bore a For Sale sign. And the agent listing it was Scott Marlowe.

I snapped a picture of it with my phone.

Chapter 17

I consulted my handy phone map of the area and discovered Marlowe & Co. Estate Agents was only a few streets away. No time like the present. I headed in that direction. Scott Marlowe's name had come up in a couple of my inquiries, so I knew he'd been around at the time. And maybe he could shed some light on why his parents had reacted in such different ways at the mention of Mark Cardrick.

An ultra polite receptionist said Mr. Marlowe was on a conference call but it should be ending in a few minutes, if I cared to wait. I smiled and assured her that would be fine.

I may have shown her the photo I'd snapped of the house with their sign out front … it may have given her the impression I was here to talk about a deal. Scott Marlowe seemed to think so when he walked out to the reception area with a beaming smile and extended his hand.

He had his mother's coloring—the blonde hair and creamy complexion seemed more fitting somehow on a woman. He wore dark slacks, white dress shirt, and a tie with a tiny pattern of ducks that could easily be taken for misshapen polka dots. His physique ran more like his father's—chunky around the middle—although Scott's was due more likely to a rich diet than to age. I placed him in his early fifties.

"I understand you are inquiring about the Scofield house, Miss …" Obviously, he didn't remember me from our brief passing at the bookshop.

"Charlie Parker. Actually, could we talk in your office?" I followed him past an alcove with a kettle and tea setup, declining the beverage offer when he asked.

His office was a small room, neatly furnished, but with nothing remarkable about it. Standard desk, chairs, and bookcases from whatever was the equivalent of Office Max here, hardly the impression of a business mogul. One wall had a map of Bury and the nearby area with red and blue pushpins stuck in random places—most likely where the company had listed or sold a property. Scott's desk faced it, and I imagined it as his own personal scoreboard. Behind his desk, for the visitor to see, was a framed photo of the English countryside and a hilltop castle in the distance. Maybe that was another facet of Marlowe's vision for himself.

"I found your office address from one of your listings, but what I really want to talk about is something from the past." I gave my now-standard spiel about my investigating a missing person. "I spoke with your parents after learning they may have known the man."

I brought up Cardrick's photo on my phone and handed it to him.

"Really. And who are we talking about? Who is this man?"

"His name is Mark Cardrick, an American. He was living briefly here in Bury before he vanished. His sister filed a missing person report in her home state, but they were unable to track Mark any farther than his initial arrival in London. A few people here recall seeing him after that date, here in Bury."

A muscle in his jaw worked as he looked at the photo. "Afraid I can't be of any help at all," he said, handing back my phone.

"Your father told me he didn't recognize Cardrick, but your mother seemed to remember him quite well."

Scott's expression changed. "Ah, yes, well. My father is nearing eighty and has been experiencing memory problems for years. Whatever he tells you today can change tomorrow. And Mum isn't a whole lot better. What, exactly, did she say?"

"She commented that Cardrick was very attractive."

"See? Exactly what I meant. She looked at this photo and said the man was attractive. I could say the same. In Mum's mind, Michael Bublé and Sean Connery are also attractive men. Did she actually say she had met him? Trust me, she's never met Sean Connery."

Technically true—I couldn't remember *exactly* what Sarah had said. I felt a little put off. "So, are you saying she's never met Mark Cardrick either? He lived in an apartment right above their bookstore."

He shrugged. "I wouldn't know."

"And while we're parsing words, can you say for certain

that you've never met him either?"

"That's just what I'm saying. Look, I hate to cut this short, but I have another meeting in ten minutes. My parents may have met this fellow, maybe not. I'm just saying their memories that far back won't be reliable. And now I really must leave to show a house." He stood, clearly showing me the door.

Outside the office, I lingered and watched him drive away in a yellow Mini. What kind of real estate mogul drives a Mini? Anyway, it looked as though I was back to square one. I was making no headway whatsoever with this.

Back at Louisa's I set up my computer and went online to the Sleuths International website again. Logging in, I sent a message to coldcasehannah.

Moments later, I had a reply. Was just about to text you. Found more info on our Mr. Cardrick. It's juicy!

Chapter 18

We met in the lobby of the Angel Hotel. In person, coldcasehannah — actually Hannah Case — was about my age, a petite blonde with a bright smile. She'd scooped her shoulder-length hair up into a clip, and she wore a denim skirt and pink T-shirt with three buttons across one shoulder. She popped up from the overstuffed chair she'd occupied and shook my hand.

"You're Charlie. You look exactly like your voice."

We'd spoken on the phone to make our meeting plan. There was no way I was seeing an online contact in person without a preliminary conversation, and I had to admit to myself Hannah looked just like her voice too. We both laughed a little over it.

She glanced around the lobby, where a group of older ladies occupied one cluster of couches and chairs, and a lone businessman had staked out another while he apparently waited for someone to join him.

"Want to grab a glass of wine or something?" Hannah asked. "There's a super cute bar here, and I imagine it's not crowded just yet. We might have a bit more privacy there." She tucked a leather portfolio under one arm and pointed to an alcove off the lobby where a sign above a door said Wingspan.

We walked down a short set of steps into what must have, at one point in history, been a wine cellar, a keep, or a dungeon. Stone arches divided the room into sections that wound around corners and provided several cozy niches, revealed by recessed lighting. Pendant lights highlighted the bar which, on closer examination, I realized was the wing of a small airplane. The tables were fashioned from old engine cowlings, and wooden propellers hung on the walls. Movie posters from World War II films showed scenes of diving airplanes and sported titles like "Wings of Valor" and "Bullets Over Britain."

I'd been so busy gawking Hannah had to nudge me to ask about my drink. She'd asked for a glass of white wine for herself, so I made mine the same. She pulled a handful of crumpled bills from her pocket and dropped one of them on the bar. "My treat," she said.

We chose a table around a corner from the bar and main section of the room. The only other customers at this early hour were a couple who obviously wanted privacy in one of the small niches and two banker types who'd taken seats on stools facing the wing-bar. Settling in, we covered what each of us did in real life—she was a hair stylist and this was her early afternoon off.

"I took an interest in cold cases when I learned a

childhood friend of Mum's had vanished and no one ever knew what happened. Of course, the parents were devastated and refused to believe their daughter wouldn't come walking back in one day. When I learned this, they'd already passed on, still having faith, but our Sleuths International group was able to locate some clues. The little girl's remains were found in a shallow grave not three kilometers from her home."

"So sad."

"Yes, it was. Since then I've kept this keen interest in learning more." She sipped her wine and stared toward one of the stone arches for a moment. "However—now I've got children of my own, I can't handle the emotion surrounding crimes against children. Sorry, just can't do it. I've developed a bit of a specialty in cases involving con artists. Unbelievably, the police often let those go. I don't know if it's the idea that the victims are somehow to blame for letting themselves be conned, or what. Myself, it makes me want to throttle the perpetrators, or at least see them locked up for a good long time."

"Especially since they tend to prey on the elderly or others who really can't afford to lose what little they have."

"Exactly." She reached for her portfolio and unzipped the cover. "Which is why I was very interested to learn that your missing man—now deceased—was quite the con artist."

"Really." I felt my interest perk up.

"One of his specialties was known as the heir-finder con." She met my gaze, keeping a finger tucked into the pages of the notebook. "I don't know if you've studied this much?"

I shook my head.

"There are basically two styles of con games—the short con and the long con. The short con happens quickly, on the spot. 'Hey, buddy, if you'll advance me two hundred dollars to claim my grandmother's diamond ring, we'll sell it and split the profits. I've already got an offer on the table for twenty thousand, but I need to get the ring from the pawn shop.' The victim hands over two hundred dollars, believing he'll end up with ten thousand. The con man goes into the pawn shop and out the back door, and the poor man out front never sees him or his money again."

"Wow."

"That's a short con. The long con can run for days, weeks, even years. It takes a lot of planning, but the stakes are greater. Remember the movie, *The Sting*? That was a long con. Cleaning out someone's entire bank account, taking their home, bilking them repeatedly the way gypsy fortune tellers can do ... Those are long cons."

"And Mark Cardrick was into which style?"

"We've found evidence to suggest some of each. He met women during his travels. One even paid for a sports car, and another bought him one of those pricey racing motorcycles. At the very least, it seems they paid all his expenses and bought him fine clothing."

Louisa. An uneasy flutter started in my stomach.

"He was here in Bury St. Edmunds, where some of our members believe he was trying to set up this heir-finder scam."

At my puzzled expression, she continued. "The basic version is that someone shows up, saying they've located you as the long-lost relative of Uncle ... someone. Your uncle had no other heirs and his entire fortune will come to you. In the version that's slightly legitimate, there really is an inheritance—the con man has learned this from public records. He's going to bring you forth as the real heir, and if there's money to be had, he takes a huge fee for his part in getting it for you. But the other version is far more common. The so-called heir-finder declares that in order to receive your inheritance, you'll need to come up with a series of bank fees, legal expenses, and so forth. He may start small so you'll believe for a few hundred dollars you'll receive hundreds of thousands. Once a victim has invested something, he has a much higher emotional attachment to the outcome and the dream that his inheritance is right around the corner.

"These days, the internet is a huge help to these criminals. They set up fake websites to represent the fake bank, the rich uncle's social media pages, even law firms the con man claims represent the estate. It can be quite convincing."

"And back then? In the early '90s the internet wasn't nearly what it is today."

"Right. So, it was done with forged papers and a winning personality."

"Cardrick definitely had the winning personality."

"So we've heard." She opened the portfolio and brought out some pages. "These are photocopies of documents we located where the supposed deceased rich relative was a William Parker."

"My father?"

She stared. "My gosh. Was it?"

"That was his name. And he passed away … No, I think the timeframe isn't right. I'm not sure." My head was spinning.

"But if Mark Cardrick brought up that name to Louisa

Parker, it might have been the reason the police interviewed her at the time he went missing."

The flutter in my stomach threatened to upend the lunch I'd eaten hours ago. I needed to talk to Louisa.

Chapter 19

I thanked Hannah and we promised to keep in touch but, truthfully, I couldn't get out of the Wingspan bar and the hotel quickly enough. Out on the front sidewalk I took a deep breath as Hannah walked toward her small car. The tourism office was just across the parking lot and up the street a short way. Could I catch Louisa there? Should I try?

I glanced left and right and thought I spotted her, rounding the corner toward Abbeygate Street. I dashed up the sidewalk in pursuit. Her flowing purple skirt gave her away, and I called out her name. She turned and waited for me.

"Well, hello, darling. Were you out looking for me? I should have texted you to make plans."

"No—well, actually I met up with a lady for drinks. The sleuthing group I might have mentioned … Look, we need to talk."

I glanced up and saw Brody's Tea Shop just ahead. Maybe if I got Louisa in the area where the old bones had been found, I'd see how she reacted. And then maybe I could get her to concentrate on answering questions about Mark. I took her elbow firmly and steered her toward the door.

Alva was placing chairs upside down on the table tops, preparing to mop. "We're closed." Then she saw it was me. "Oh, Charlie. Sorry, I've already put away—"

"It's fine. We just need to take a look in there for a minute. No more than five, I promise." I still had Louisa's arm in my grip.

She wanted to bolt, I could tell it, but she wouldn't cause a scene. I pushed aside the plastic curtain and we stepped into the vacant room. Louisa came to a stop, rubbed her temples, and began to walk slowly toward the remains of the stone stairs at the back wall. I let go of her. The broken red bricks had been hauled away. A stack of lumber sat nearby, most likely in readiness for framing in the space.

"Talk to me," I said.

Her eyes closed and she pressed a finger to the spot between her eyebrows. "Such spirit activity here. It's noisy with voices. Women and men, dishes clattering. It's a tavern or something."

"It was, at one time, but that was long ago. Do you have memories of this place? Personal memories of being here?"

She looked at me, bright-eyed and clear. "No. But ..." She stared at the room, calculating dimensions. "The flat where I lived—where Mark lived with me for awhile—was directly above this place, wasn't it?"

I had guessed as much.

"His spirit was here for a very long time," she said softly. "But I sense that it's gone now. He's been freed somehow. No, not quite. He's nearly free."

"His killer hasn't been caught," I said, keeping my voice low. "Do you have any sense of who might have done it?"

She shook her head. "I don't."

I believed her. I remembered her comment, back in London, how she'd learned at the symposium that sometimes spirits assisted in solving crimes. It seemed no easy answers of that sort would happen here today.

"I learned some interesting new things about Mark this afternoon," I told her. "Can we talk about that on the way home?"

Alva was working near the opening. I could see her bright yellow mop bucket through the translucent plastic; back-and-forth movement caught my eye, and it was obvious she was trying to eavesdrop.

I swept the curtain back and smiled at Alva. "We'll be going now. Thanks for your time."

Out on the street, we walked a block before either of us said anything. Louisa looked somewhat drained. I linked her hand over my arm and patted it.

"That place back there and the memories of Mark—that wasn't easy, was it?"

"Oh, Charlie, such a long time ago." She took a deep breath, drew her free hand through the fronds of a hanging fern at a lamppost, and got some of her color back.

"I have to ask you … Did your breakup with Mark result from his trying to pull some kind of scam? Did he say anything about an inheritance from your brother or anything?"

"No, not my brother. Bill was still alive back then. But there was an uncle on the Parker side with the same first name. Mark had somehow got that information. There was a whole business about my standing to inherit a lot of money or some such. I knew it was untrue, right from the start. None of the Parkers had wealth. Your father was the first to attend college. Most of them were uneducated fundamentalists."

"And is that what you meant when you said you and Mark 'had words' before he left?"

We passed the Corn Exchange, ignoring a favorite restaurant in the same block.

"Anything else? I'm really just trying to narrow this down to what the police might look at if they get this far in their investigation. What happened after the argument that led to his moving out?"

"He left. I never saw him again, not even walking about town. I assumed he'd gone back to richer grounds around the Mediterranean."

"Richer women, maybe?"

She gave me a knowing look. "Of course. I might have been young and free-spirited, Charlie, but I wasn't completely stupid. He played women for whatever he could get. I had nothing, so we simply had fun."

"How did he think he could get money out of you for the inheritance scam?"

"I have no idea. I mean, I truly didn't understand how it all worked, in his mind. Maybe there was some chap somewhere in America called Parker who'd left a fortune and no heirs. Maybe that's how Mark thought we could claim a fortune? If he convinced me I was the true heir, I wouldn't be able to break down and admit being a part of the con, now could I?"

I had probably underestimated her. Her woo-woo beliefs in ghosts and spirits aside, my aunt had a pretty level head on her shoulders.

I went to bed that night feeling the relief that comes from full certainty that my aunt had nothing to do with a murder. Still, someone had killed Mark Cardrick and it would be in the Parker family's best interests if I could ferret out that person before the police came too strongly after Louisa.

The list of potential suspects ran through my head. They were mainly the women I'd spoken with—Angelica, Clarice, and Sarah—and it seemed almost ludicrous to imagine any of them as murderers. But I had to remind myself they weren't always grandmothers and soft-spoken shop owners. As a womanizer, Mark had no doubt hurt several, wounded the pride of others. Angelica had very purposely steered me toward Clarice. Sarah seemed so motherly and unassuming, but she had closed down at some of my questions. For that matter, Alva Brody had shut down when the body was found.

One item seemed significant. Someone had mentioned Mark's having frequent business at the bank. What could that be about? Maybe he'd already collected on previous cons, or maybe he was working one and needed access to ready funds. I could probably go back and ask questions and perhaps get the name of the bank he'd used, but the likelihood that I could walk into the bank now and ask to see records on a customer, even one from ages back—nah, I couldn't see myself getting anywhere with that.

Still, I thought as I turned out the light and rolled over, the more information I could gather, the more I could turn over to the police. They *would* be able to gain access to bank records. On that note, I snuggled into my pillow and drifted off.

Chapter 20

Louisa was bustling about the kitchen when I went downstairs in the morning.

"I'm leading my tour tonight," she told me. She was plucking items from a cardboard box, taking hold of something with silk flowers and ribbon streamers. "It's summer solstice, so I'm taking the group through the old Abbey ruins by moonlight. The ghost of Saint Edmund should be particularly active—he usually is at the full moon."

I chuckled and poured myself a mug of coffee from her ancient percolator. "I'm sure he will be."

"Do come with us, Charlie. It's great fun, poking about in the moonlight, especially when we arrive at the graveyard and I take them to the crypt and tell the story of the Grey Lady."

I debated. It might be interesting. Something I would never get to do at home, and midnight in a graveyard is probably on everyone's bucket list, right?

My phone pinged with a message, saving me from giving an immediate answer.

"Oh, no," popped out of me before I could think. "It's the airline, confirming my flight home day after tomorrow." I had become so wrapped up in this idyllic little town and the mystery I'd been working on that I had nearly forgotten about being on a schedule.

"Then it's perfect," Louisa said. "Tonight's your big chance to meet Saint Edmund and the Grey Lady."

She shook the beribboned circlet in her hand and placed it on her head, becoming a spritely little figure wearing a crown of flowers and a veil of ribbons.

Absentmindedly, I nodded agreement while reviewing my flight information. A message from Drake came through. He'd worked it out so his break would coincide with my arrival home. He sounded excited. And although I was eager to see him and to have our little family back together again, I felt antsy. I really wanted to stick around here until I had answers to the questions about the bones in the stairwell, and could leave with the assurance that Louisa wasn't going to be caught under the police department's magnifying glass.

At the very least, I felt I should share the information I'd gathered so far and steer them in the direction of coldcasehannah and the sleuthing group. I looked up the number and placed a call to the station, asking for either Edwards or Redding. Both, I was told, were out on a case. Could someone else help me? Probably not. Would an appointment at three p.m. be acceptable?

The politeness was nearly overwhelming—of course, I accepted the appointment time.

Meanwhile, I spent the morning doing what I'd intended at the beginning of my trip, heading to the shops to pick up gifts to take home and then trying to fit it all into my luggage. Sooner than I could have imagined, it was two-thirty.

I didn't bother changing out of my jeans, but I did take the time to brush my hair and gather the photocopies Hannah had left with me. Although she also intended to share the information with the police, I figured I had no use for the extra paperwork once I went back to the States. What I hoped to gain from the meeting with the cops was to see if they had a file on confidence games in this area, then maybe put it together from one of the victims' complaints whether Mark Cardrick was the perp. From there, a name might jump out as the probable killer, and I would instantly become a hero in local British police work.

Right.

I set out on foot and arrived at seven minutes before three. Unfortunately, Edwards and Redding had been detained somewhere and didn't come along until nearly four o'clock. It turned out the Bury police department was fairly small, so it wasn't as if there were scads of other detectives or a bunco squad or someone else to turn to. Meanwhile, a pleasant receptionist had given me tea and a tasty little butter cookie, so I could hardly complain about being forced to wait.

I had my spiel ready, rattled off the basics of the inheritance scam, and quickly got to the part about their recent case, pointing out that it involved a known con man as the victim. "I was hoping you had a file on him. Surely, if someone here in town had fallen for his line they would have reported it."

"Unfortunately," said DS Redding, "victims of confidence games often do exactly the opposite. They feel embarrassed and don't want their gullibility known."

Sadly, it made sense. "But someone who felt they had no other option might have gotten angry enough with him to kill him."

I was afraid my suggestion would fall on deaf ears, but both detectives perked up.

"Motive is always an important part of the puzzle," Edwards said.

I wanted so badly to let them know I'd already eliminated Louisa—at least in my own mind—as a suspect, but bringing up her name might be all the prompting they would need to begin looking more seriously at her. I ran a dozen phrases through my mind, but before I could settle on the right one, Redding's desk phone rang.

Whatever the caller said got their attention. They excused themselves politely but quickly and ushered me out.

"Thank you for your efforts, Miss Parker. We'll pursue your idea as time permits."

Well, darn. Clearly they weren't in a huge hurry on this, and Mark Cardrick's death was still barely above a cold case to them. I took the shortcut toward the town center and was midway through the graveyard when I remembered one of the most important things I'd meant to add to the conversation. The banking angle. One of my interviewees had said Mark often had business at the bank, and I'd intended to mention it to the police so they could check it out.

I started to turn back, but what was the point? The two detectives had left. I could phone them—Edwards had left his business card with me. I came out near the Norman Tower and was about to cross Crown Street, mulling the connections between Mark and the money, when a thought struck me. My heart began to beat faster. I zigzagged to the right and headed toward Marlowe's Books.

Chapter 21

It was nearly closing time and the lights inside the shop cast a soft glow through the front windows. The faster I walked, the quicker my thoughts processed. Someone had told me the bookshop was once on the brink of bankruptcy and had made a turn-around. Where had that money come from? Could old Mr. Marlowe have been in cahoots with Cardrick and collected on one of his scams?

I paused outside and stared through the windows. It was nearly closing time. A customer with a stack of paperbacks stood at the counter, handing a credit card to Sarah. There didn't appear to be any other patrons inside. I walked in, smiled toward Sarah, and made my way to the back where I made sure no one was in the children's section or the reference area.

When the bells above the door tinkled, I strolled up to the desk.

"Good afternoon, Charlie. Are you still enjoying your visit?" She was only half aware of me as she pulled out a calculator and added numbers from some old-fashioned paper receipts.

"It's been good. Sadly, I have to leave soon, so I'm tying up some loose ends about Mark Cardrick. Can I ask you something?"

It wasn't in her nature to be rude, so she looked up and smiled.

"Someone told me Mr. Cardrick had a business in which he helped locate missing heirs. I wonder if that subject ever came up when you knew him?"

"Oh, yes. That's exactly what he talked with Clive about."

I hadn't expected her to sound quite so happy about it. "In what way?"

She turned her eyes upward, thinking. "Well, it seems there was a great-aunt … What was her name …? Penelope or Persephone or something …"

I might have let out a tiny, impatient sound.

"No matter what her name was. She'd left a decent-sized estate that had gone unclaimed. Mark's company had tracked the lineage and found Clive was the nearest relative and therefore had a claim on the money."

"Were you asked to pay a fee or taxes or anything, in order to receive the money?"

Her mouth formed a little twist. "No, not that I recall. Wouldn't have done any good. We had less than nothing, I mean, with the shop debt and all. No, I'm quite certain we didn't have to pay anything in advance."

"So, no money in advance … what happened then?"

"As I recall, some time went by, maybe a few weeks,

a few months. Heavens, it's been too long to remember those details. But after a time, the money came through. Went directly into our bank account, I believe."

According to all the info I'd heard on these scams, no one ever actually received any money. Had Cardrick given them something, maybe as seed money or a lure to reel in someone else—a bigger fish?

"You mentioned the estate was 'a decent size'? I'm guessing you didn't become instant millionaires or anything." I gestured around the unpretentious shop.

"Oh heavens no. We paid all the debts, moved the shop from rented quarters to this location, which we purchased, and took care of some things at home. We've become very fortunate that we can now work for the pleasure of being around books, and we enjoy our customers. I imagine I'll be behind this desk forever, and I love it that way."

"Good for you. I'm happy to hear it." Puzzled, but glad it worked out for her.

"Yes, the inheritance came at the right moment. I only wish we'd known this aunt in time to appreciate her company."

The bells at the door jingled again and I looked up. Clive and his son had walked in.

"Good evening, Miss Parker," Scott said. "I'm glad to have run into you. There's a property we should discuss. Let's speak outside. Please?"

In a flash, the whole picture unfolded.

He'd taken my elbow and guided me toward the door. "I'll see you tomorrow, Mum," he called over his shoulder as he gave me a little shove down the steps to the sidewalk.

"What the hell?" I demanded. "This isn't about real estate."

"I'm the one who should be asking what the bloody hell. You come round here speaking to my mother about their financial status?"

He'd walked me past the bookshop so we couldn't be observed from inside. The next shop over was a butcher's, and it was already closed for the night. In fact, as I glanced around, most of the stores had closed and there were few people on the street.

"Well? What were you bothering Mum about?"

A buzzing sound started in my ears as the pieces began to fall into place. "Nothing at all. She offered the information that it was an inheritance which allowed them to move to this street and to keep the shop open all these years. But there's more, isn't there? Mark Cardrick came around, talking about an inheritance from a relative your parents never knew. It was a scam—one Cardrick was known to have pulled on others. How did they actually get the money?" My heart began to pound.

His eyes darted up the street. "I've got some interesting information about that at my office. Come on, I can show you. My car's right here." He pointed to the yellow Mini I'd seen him driving the other day.

There was no way I was getting into a car with him at the wheel. I grabbed the strap of my shoulder bag and whipped it toward him, whacking the side of his head Then I ran.

Chapter 22

I hadn't managed to knock him down, merely to make him furious. Scott's heavy footsteps pounded the sidewalk behind me and I realized it had been a while since I'd done any serious exercise. He was catching up fast.

Options were running slim. All the shops were dark now. A block down, just around the corner, I remembered a restaurant. If I could get inside, he surely wouldn't follow and cause a scene.

But before I'd even reached the corner, I felt a hand on my shoulder. His breath rasped in my ear.

I turned on him, dropping my bag and grabbing his wrist. Dimly aware of a car rounding the corner, some kind of muscle memory kicked in and I remembered a move Ron had once taught me. I shifted my weight, twisted his arm backward and managed to pull his wrist up behind his back. He let out a howl.

I was breathing so hard I was seeing speckles, but there was no way I was letting go of him now. I pushed him against the plaster wall of a clothing store and looked around, trying to figure out what to do next.

Scott ranted. "Bloody bookstore! Don't want the stupid place, never did." He stood with his forehead to the wall, wailing. At least he wasn't fighting me, but I didn't trust that he wouldn't turn on me if I eased my grip.

The oncoming car had pulled to the curb and two figures jumped out. I nearly cried with relief when I realized it was the police.

DC Edwards reached me. "What's all this? Charlie Parker?" He was always the slower of the two.

DS Redding took in the scene and already had cuffs in hand. "Handy that you've got Scott Marlowe here, miss. We was just headed to his office to talk with him."

"Really?" I gladly relinquished the suspect to them and began looking for my purse, which had landed twenty feet away.

"What you said about the con man and his inheritance scam," said Redding. "Something from the past clicked with me. I'd actually suspected the old man of somehow stealing the money. Your coming up with the son was brilliant."

It was, no doubt, the best compliment I would ever receive from the British constabulary, even though it was slightly inaccurate.

Redding clamped handcuffs on Scott. "Scott Marlowe, you are under arrest. You do not have to say anything …"

They turned to me. "We'll take it from here," Edwards said, and they marched Scott to the waiting cruiser.

The light was fading fast as I walked home to Louisa's. She was in the shower but I found a sandwich she'd left for me on a plate in the kitchen. Her flower crown and something that looked like a laser light stick sat on the table, no doubt the props she used in her haunted tours presentation.

I had completely forgotten my promise to go along.

By the time she came downstairs, I'd eaten only two bites of the sandwich, and although my mind was whirling with unanswered questions about the murder that was at least a step or two closer to being solved, I didn't see how I could resolve them by sitting home all evening. I changed into a clean shirt and jeans and got out my lightweight jacket.

"All set then?" she asked, picking up her things.

I would only be here another day—I couldn't disappoint her. We set out toward the meeting point where ticket-holders-only were allowed inside the Abbey Gardens after dark. Beneath the arch of the ancient Abbey Gate, Louisa began with stories of the burning of the original gate and the spirits who lingered in the area.

I trailed along but no matter how I tried to concentrate on the names and places she spoke of, my mind was still reeling with the events of the afternoon and the unanswered questions. I could imagine—now that I thought about it—Scott's anger toward the man who was trying to cheat his father. Most likely the money Mark Cardrick was trying to wheedle from Clive Marlowe would put them over the edge financially, causing them to lose their business and probably anything Scott might hope for in the way of college tuition or real estate schooling. So, okay, I understood the rage that could have driven a hotheaded twenty-year-old.

A night bird swooped through the garden, bringing shrieks from Louisa's group. She laughed, saying it must be the spirit of the Grey Lady coming by to say hello.

I only had one day remaining here, and I hate loose ends. I decided to stop by the police station in the morning to see if I could visit the suspect. It was all I could do for now, so I shifted my attention back to my aunt and her stories.

It was fun to watch her with an audience, animated and cute in her flowing outfit as she waved her pointer toward one spot after another—a high clerestory window in the Abbey where she said the face of a young vicar could be seen sometimes, a corner of the herb garden where it was rumored the bones of an ancient druid rose to visit the real world on moonlit nights. I found myself edging closer to the group; I'd just about had my fill of old bones for now.

The tour concluded at the stroke of midnight, on the street near the Norman Gate, after Louisa had entertained us with the highlights of the headstone inscriptions in the ancient graveyard. She and I walked home afterward. Clearly in her element with her audience and presentation, she needed the brisk walk to dissipate her excess energy.

Chapter 23

The morning visit to the jail felt almost anti-climactic after the drama of the previous evening's capture. Scott Marlowe sat on the edge of his metal-framed bed, wearing his same slacks and shirt from last night—minus belt and shoes. His expression told me he was still in shock over the turn of events. He must have become quite comfortable in his life as a successful real estate agent and probably never dreamed he would be held accountable for his actions from decades past.

Louisa came with me. We'd sat up into the wee hours, and I'd filled her in on what I had learned about Mark's death. She told me she'd left that part of her life behind a very long time ago. Still, I could tell she felt something. Regret, maybe, that Mark had followed her to Bury and that he had upended so many lives here.

Constable Edwards accepted my explanation that we only wanted to ask a few questions of the suspect. The police had already pieced together much of the story, and Edwards told me Scott hadn't denied any of it. He stood to one side when Louisa and I approached Scott's cell.

"*Why*, Scott?" Louisa blurted before anyone else said a word. "Why would you?" Tears filled her eyes and she gripped the bars, trying to shake them. The emotion she'd held back for so long came rushing to the surface.

Scott ignored her cries and glared at me as though it was all my fault he was sitting here. When Louisa repeated her plea he rushed toward her, roaring like a caged tiger.

Edwards stepped forward and took Louisa's arm. "Ma'am, let's step outside." He gently guided her toward his office.

I gave one final look at Scott Marlowe, any regret I might have felt over dredging up the old situation vanishing now. He felt no remorse for his crime. If anything, it seemed he thought he had been completely entitled to his freedom simply because he'd gotten away with it so long.

At Edwards's desk, I asked the questions that had been bothering me.

"How did he manage to hide the body and get away with it?"

"What we've pieced together during the investigation showed the murder happened during a previous renovation of the shop space. The shoe store had closed, so the half of the MacCallum building was sitting empty. We think Marlowe got Mr. Cardrick to meet him there, probably on the pretense that he would hand over the money Cardrick wanted from the parents. There was no opening between the bookshop and the empty space at the time, obviously, so their meeting could have been conducted in privacy."

I could picture all of that. "But what about the stairs? Those stone steps were there a very long time, weren't they? So, I'm guessing the brick wall that was just torn down this week wasn't there at the time?"

"Correct. The old stairs had just sat there for ages, even though the top had been sealed off when flats were added above and access to them was gained by outdoor stairs at the back, rather than giving tenants access through the shop below."

Louisa was nodding. "Yes, that's how it was back then."

"And so … what? Scott added the brick wall?" I tried to picture this kid, barely out of his teens, doing that.

"Yes. Bragged about it, in fact. He'd held jobs for construction companies during his summer breaks. He boasted to me last night what a great bricklayer he was."

"Okay." I must have raised an eyebrow.

"We think he may have salvaged the bricks from some other job, or he may have contacted a supplier with a fake order and had them delivered. He probably doused the body with quick lime and proceeded to build the wall. It will all come out at his trial, certainly."

And he'd been lucky that no other tenant moved into the empty shop right away to report the smell of decomposition.

"I suppose my big question is the money. The elder Marlowes said they actually did receive an inheritance from this imaginary uncle Mark Cardrick told them about. But the uncle didn't exist and the money didn't exist … How did they get it?"

"We're still working out that bit. My partner is at the bank right now, getting their computer records, but here's what we think. After Scott struck the victim and shoved the body into the stairwell area, he must have rummaged through the man's pockets. There was no wallet or identification in the clothing when we recovered the remains. Most likely our killer was able to get everything he needed—a safe deposit box key, something with the man's signature on it, perhaps some kind of passcode to get into Cardrick's banking records. At any rate, we believe Cardrick had someplace to stash money he'd collected from other victims—perhaps he'd even bragged about it to Scott. We don't know how well they knew each other.

"After hiding the body, Scott probably cleared the safe deposit box or account, using Cardrick's credentials. Showing up with the money to help his parents assured that they would never question Cardrick's story, nor would they feel any obligation toward turning the money in … it was theirs, so far as they knew."

Wow. Such a twisted tale that ultimately had fairly simple answers. I thanked the policeman for sharing the information. I could now go home, relieved Louisa wasn't in danger of being dragged into the whole mess. She was quiet as we left the station.

As we walked by Marlowe's Books, I wondered what would happen to the family. Clive and Sarah had built the bookshop on the hope that it would become their son's passion, a legacy he could continue in their names. But surely they had realized the store wasn't where his interests lay. Perhaps, as they got older, the sale of the store and of Scott's real estate business could see them comfortably into their retirement.

I saw Louisa eyeing the bookshop. "What are you thinking?" I asked.

She smiled, the old brightness back in her expression.

"Playing a little game of what-if, I suppose."

"Seriously? You could be happy running a little retail store?"

She ran a hand over the decorative window frame. "Dunno … maybe. Of course, if I were running this shop, there would have to be quite a large section of books on the history of the town and the ghosts who live here."

I laughed. "I can definitely see that."

"Oh, it's just talk. I like my part-time work, and it's fun to meet people and do my tours." She gave a final, pensive glance at the display window full of books. "Who's to say?"

True. Who could say what the future holds for any of us?

As for my immediate future, I needed to focus on packing, catching my train in the early morning tomorrow, and getting through the maze that is Heathrow so I could be on my way home to Drake and Freckles and the rest of my little circle. And I might start paying more attention to what my fortune cookies tell me.

* * *

Thank you for taking the time to read *Old Bones Can Be Murder.* If you enjoyed it, please consider telling your friends or posting a short review. Word of mouth is an author's best friend and is much appreciated.

Thank you,

Connie Shelton

Sign up for Connie Shelton's free mystery newsletter
at www.connieshelton.com
and receive advance information about new books,
along with a chance at prizes, discounts and
other mystery news!

Contact by email: connie@connieshelton.com
Follow Connie Shelton on Twitter, Pinterest,
Instagram and Facebook

www.ingramcontent.com/pod-product-compliance
Lightning Source LLC
Chambersburg PA
CBHW050539190726
48284CB00003B/1143